PRA...
MICHAE...
HIS MONSIEU...
SERIES

"Pamplemousse philanders, knows wine labels like his ABC's, and treats his canine sidekick like a human being. . . . Light, diverting, skillfully made."
—*The New York Times Book Review*

"As Maurice Chevalier might have sung of Bond's work, thank heaven for little pearls."
—*Chicago Tribune*

"Every now and then, there emerges from the crowd a fictional detective who, for one reason or another, is able to win a permanent place in the hearts of his readers. Sherlock Holmes, Father Brown, Philip Marlowe, and Perry Mason are a few examples. . . . Aristide Pamplemousse certainly must be considered a leading candidate to join that select group."
—*The San Diego Union-Tribune*

"Monsieur Pamplemousse is fabulous fare. Your table's waiting. *Bon appetit.*"
—*Raleigh News & Observer*

Also by Michael Bond
Published by Fawcett Crest:

MONSIEUR PAMPLEMOUSSE
MONSIEUR PAMPLEMOUSSE AND
    THE SECRET MISSION
MONSIEUR PAMPLEMOUSSE TAKES THE CURE
MONSIEUR PAMPLEMOUSSE ALOFT
MONSIEUR PAMPLEMOUSSE INVESTIGATES

MONSIEUR PAMPLEMOUSSE RESTS HIS CASE

Michael Bond

FAWCETT CREST • NEW YORK

A Fawcett Crest Book
Published by Ballantine Books
Copyright © 1991 by Michael Bond

Library of Congress Catalog Card Number: 91-70650

ISBN 0-449-22045-1

Manufactured in the United States of America

First Ballantine Books Hardcover Edition: November 1991
First Ballantine Books Mass Market Edition: October 1993

CONTENTS

1

HANDS ACROSS THE OCEAN

THE DIRECTOR SETTLED HIMSELF COMFORTABLY in the leather armchair behind his desk, shuffled a few papers nervously to and fro across the top, carefully covering as he did so a large map of the United States of America, then cleared his throat as he brought both hands together to form a miniature steeple with his fingertips.

Recognising the signs, Monsieur Pamplemousse sought reassurance by giving the top of Pommes Frites' head a passing pat, then sat back waiting for the worst. He wondered idly if it would be a case of being addressed by his surname or by his Christian name. From the shape of the steeple—high and severely orthodox—he guessed at the former. The Director was wearing his official look: a mixture of barely concealed disapproval and distaste of what he was about to say. He cleared his throat a second time.

1

'Pamplemousse, I have no doubt that in your previous occupation—I refer, of course, to your years with the Sûreté—you had need from time to time to consult the *Code Napoléon*?'

Monsieur Pamplemousse made a non-committal grunt. There had been more than one occasion when he would gladly have seized hold of a copy, preferably a leather-bound edition, and used it in order to batter a particularly belligerent or uncooperative offender into telling the truth, but he sensed it was neither the time nor the place to say so.

'Good.' The Director picked up a sheet of paper. 'That makes my task easier. I would like, if I may, to draw your attention to Article 1101: the definition of a contract.

'It states, and I quote: "A contract is a convention by which one or several persons commit themselves towards one or several other persons to give, to do, or not to do something."

'I'm sure you will agree that the extract I have just read is a masterpiece of construction. The wording is concise—a mere twenty-eight words; the meaning crystal clear and unassailable.'

Seeing that something more than a mere grunt was expected of him, Monsieur Pamplemousse nodded his agreement. There was no point in doing otherwise.

'I am pleased you agree, Pamplemousse. To carry matters a stage further, in accepting your present post as an Inspector with *Le Guide*, you committed yourself to a contract. Why, then, when I arrived at my office this morning, did I find a letter of resignation on my desk? I have, of course, torn it up, but I think I deserve an explanation.'

'The answer is perfectly simple, *Monsieur*. It was in

response to your memo of yesterday's date asking me to stand by for further instructions. By the merest chance I happened to be passing the Operations Room and when I went inside I saw where they had put my flag. Not, as I had every good reason to expect, in the *Section Vacances*, but lying on its side in the pending tray. The staff were unusually evasive and I began putting two and two together. It did not take me long to come up with an answer. One which, if I may say so, is certainly not covered by the *Code Napoléon*.'

The Director made a clucking noise. 'My dear Pamplemousse, everything is covered by the *Code Napoléon*. If it is not in the *Code Napoléon*, then it does not exist. In their wisdom, its authors made sure the document covered every conceivable eventuality; from the laws which govern our country, to the way one should behave when visiting a public garden; from the manner in which letters should be written— the various forms of address and the correct phrasing of salutations, down to the time it should take a *concierge* to clean her front door-step.'

He rose to his feet, went to the window, and gazed out across the esplanade towards the Hôtel des Invalides and the vast golden dome which protected its illustrious occupant from the elements.

'Were he alive today, Pamplemousse, the Emperor would not be best pleased. If one believed in such things, one might hazard a guess that he is at this very moment turning in his tomb, thus causing consternation among those tourists from all over the world who have tendered good money in order to pay their respects.'

'With equal respect, *Monsieur*, were he alive today and in my shoes I think he would have good reason

3

to be restive. The Emperor Napoléon may have covered every eventuality which he could possibly have foreseen at that period in history, but times change. Had he been born a century and a half later, and had he found himself working for *Le Guide*, he could well have had second thoughts on the subject; he might even have toyed with the idea of introducing a possible escape clause to Article 1101; an "insofar as" perhaps, or even a simple phrase like *sauf exceptions*—"with certain exceptions"; *par exemple*, requests beyond the call of duty, particularly if it had been his understanding that he was about to enjoy a well-deserved holiday with the Empress Joséphine.'

The Director heaved a sigh and turned away from the window. Clearly, as he crossed to his drinks cupboard and removed a bottle from the ice-bucket he was preparing himself for another form of attack; a diversionary move of some kind aimed at lulling his adversary into a false sense of security prior to a sudden flanking movement.

A brief glimpse of the label confirmed Monsieur Pamplemousse's suspicions. The Chief must have been expecting trouble, otherwise why would he have had a bottle of Gosset champagne chilled and at the ready when his normal preference was for Louis Roederer? The answer was simple. He knew the tastes of his staff.

'Come, come, Aristide . . . you must not take too narrow a view of life. There are wider horizons than the one which can be seen from this window, or even from wherever it was you and Madame Pamplemousse intended spending your holiday together. Horizons which have much to offer. It is my belief that if *Le Guide* is to flourish and prepare itself for entering the twenty-first century we cannot afford to stand still. We must lay the foundation stones for the future, and we must lay them now. The recent computerisation was but a first step. Now that that particular mountain has been successfully conquered, we must put our facilities and our expertise to good use. We must expand into other areas. In particular we must look towards the New World. I am sure it is what our founder, Monsieur Hippolyte Duval, would have wished.'

The Director diverted his attention momentarily towards a painting which occupied a goodly portion of the wall above his head. Following the direction of the other's gaze, Monsieur Pamplemousse couldn't help but reflect that its principal subject, depicted by the artist toying with a bowl of *moules marinières* outside a country inn, might not have looked quite so relaxed had the river which formed the background to the picture been the Hudson rather than the Marne. By all accounts he might have felt the need to keep a more watchful eye on his bicycle, chaining it to a convenient fire hydrant for a start, instead of leaving it unattended against a nearby tree.

'Others have made a stab at it. For several years now Gault-Millau have published a guide to New York—and a very good little book it is too, even though it suffers from their usual inability to avoid the *bon mot* at other people's expense. But no one on this side of the *Atlantique*, not even Michelin, has attempted a gastronomic guide to the whole country. It is an enormous, a mind-boggling task . . .'

Monsieur Pamplemousse half rose from his seat. He didn't like the turn the conversation was taking. 'You are surely not suggesting, *Monsieur*, that I should move to America? Madame Pamplemousse would never agree to it. As for Pommes Frites . . .'

Hearing his name mentioned, Pommes Frites opened one bloodshot eye and fastened it unblinkingly on the figure hovering by the drinks cabinet. It signalled his agreement in no uncertain manner to whatever point his master might be making.

'No, no, Aristide, of course not.' The Director made haste to relieve his audience of any possible misunderstanding. 'I am merely looking into the future—the very distant future. For the moment we must content ourselves with exploring the possibilities. To that end, while I was in New York recently I made contact with the publisher of an up and coming gourmet magazine—a Mrs Van Dorman. She is a charming lady, but I suspect life in the Big Apple has passed her by to some extent. She has already carved out one successful career in the perfume business. Now she finds herself heading a publishing conglomerate which has set its sights on Europe.

'We established a certain *rapport*, the upshot of which is that she has given me a long list of establishments in the USA which could well form the basis of a guide, and in return I promised her that if she was ever in this country and in need of help I would be happy to reciprocate to the best of my ability. That moment has arrived, Pamplemousse; rather sooner than expected I have to admit—it is only a matter of weeks since we first discussed the matter—but a promise is a promise and I must do my best to slot her in.'

Monsieur Pamplemousse winced. Ever since he had arrived back from America, the Director—normally a staunch upholder of all that was sacred in the French language—had taken to peppering his speech with words and phrases which would have caused even the most catholic member of the

6

Académie Française to reel back in horror had they been present. 'Slotting things in' was the least of his transgressions. Ideas had become 'creative concepts', and 'potentials' were constantly being 'maximised'.

'It is her first visit to Europe and I can think of no one better qualified to act as her guide and mentor while she is in La Belle France than your good self. I would take on the task myself, but alas . . .' The Director raised his hands in despair. 'It is one of the problems of going away, Aristide. There are a thousand things to catch up on . . . planning next year's edition of *Le Guide* . . . making sure those who qualify receive their annual increments.' He paused for a moment. 'I believe your own salary comes up for review quite soon . . .'

Monsieur Pamplemousse stared at the Director's reflection in the mirrored interior of the cupboard. At least he had the grace to concentrate on the task in hand—the removal of the cork, silently and expertly, and the pouring of the champagne, tasks which kept his head bowed, thus enabling him to avoid a direct meeting of the eyes.

'What I am suggesting is surely not so outrageous? It could be a pleasant break from routine.'

'Madame Pamplemousse will certainly consider it outrageous, *Monsieur*. She will say I am an Inspector, not a tour guide.

'And what of the language problem?'

'Mrs Van Dorman has a little French, I believe. Enough. Besides, it does not seem to have hampered you in the past. What you cannot put into words you manage to convey all too successfully by whatever other means are at your disposal. What was the name of that English woman in the Hautes Pyrénées? Madame Cosgrove? As I recall, inhibitions were somewhat thrown to the wind on that occasion; lack of a common language did not prove to be an insurmountable barrier.'

Monsieur Pamplemousse chose to ignore the remark. Instead he tried another tack.

'I have to take my car into a blacksmith for a major repair, *Monsieur*.'

'A blacksmith, Pamplemousse?'

'I am having trouble with one of the doors. It has to do with the hinges. As you know, it is an early *deux chevaux* and the particular part is in short supply. I have been teaching Madame Pamplemousse to drive and it is not easy. We had an encounter with a *camion* in the rue Marcadet. As you may know, it is a one-way street. Unfortunately we were travelling in the wrong direction . . .'

'Why is it, Pamplemousse, that whenever you don't wish to go somewhere there is always trouble with your car? I sometimes suspect you use it as an excuse. It's high time you either bought a new one or made use of a company car like everyone else. Anyway, it will have to wait.'

'I did promise Doucette I would try and slot her in for another lesson this week in preparation for our holiday, *Monsieur*.'

The Director eyed him suspiciously as he returned to his chair. He placed two long-stemmed glasses on the desk, motioning Monsieur Pamplemousse to help himself.

'Many people would consider my proposal a signal honour, Aristide. But perhaps I haven't explained myself sufficiently well.'

Drinking deeply from his glass, he uncovered the map and set about the task of unfolding it. 'America is a large country; land of boundless opportunity.

'So far I have only tasted the delights of *La Grande Pomme*, but I cannot wait to savour other areas. New York is an exciting city, of course: a mixture of extremes. There are undercurrents which are hard to put a finger on, let alone explain. But in the same way that Paris cannot be called France, neither is New York the be all and end all of the New World. *Amérique du Nord* isn't all hamburgers with French fries on the side . . .'

'I understand they also have frankfurters, *Monsieur* . . . and doughnuts.'

'Don't be so chauvinistic, Pamplemousse. It is unworthy of you. It ignores the fact that they also have *homards* from Maine, red snappers from the Gulf of Mexico, crayfish from Louisiana, salmon from Oregon, prawns from Monterey, suckling pigs from Amador County, beef from Texas, and wines from the Napa Valley . . . the list is endless.

'They also, I may say, possess boundless enthusiasm for whatever project they happen to be involved in; a quality many of us would do well to emulate.' The Director paused in order to allow the implied criticism time to reach its target and sink in.

'Currently, Pamplemousse, as I am sure you know, there is a fashion in certain gastronomic circles for re-creating some of the great meals of the past—both in fact and fiction. The worst excesses of *nouvelle cuisine* are now behind us and people are turning to their history books.

'I understand there is a restaurant in London which has re-created on more than one occasion the meal on which the film *Babette's Feast* was based. I, myself, was lucky enough to be present only recently at a very grand occasion in the Bois de Boulogne when a whole bevy of chefs, Robuchon, Lenôtre,

9

Dutournier, and others, prepared a Pre-Revolutionary Banquet at the behest of one of the great Champagne houses.

'But when it comes to the grand gesture, the kind of function where money is no object, then one has to hand it to our friends on the other side of the Atlantic. In order to achieve their objective the question of money doesn't arise. In 1973 the Culinary Institute of America held a feast commemorating Sherlock Holmes at which a hundred guests sat down to a feast of some thirteen courses culled from the works of Conan Doyle.

'It is a quest of this nature which brings Mrs Van Dorman to our shores and she has sought my advice. She is acting as escort to a group of American crime writers who have a particular interest in culinary matters. They are members of a very élite society—*Le Cercle de Six*. They meet only once a year and on each occasion they choose a different venue.

'Last year it was Death Row in Alcatraz. The year before that they diced with the possibility of their own demise by eating fugu fish in Tokyo. This time it is the turn of Vichy.'

'Vichy?' Monsieur Pamplemousse looked at his chief in surprise.

'That seems a very odd choice, *Monsieur*. With all due respect to the chefs of that estimable city, some of whom have a place in *Le Guide*, I do not recall Stock Pots lying thick on the ground. People usually go there for the waters. They are more concerned with not eating rather than the reverse.'

'The good chefs of Vichy may well surprise us, Aristide. It could be that they will seize the opportunity with both hands. Think what it must be like to spend one's life cooking for people whose main preoccupation lies in the contemplation of their liver. How they must long to be able to tear up their calorie charts, throw caution to the wind, add a little extra cream here, another slab of *beurre* there, and indulge themselves just for once . . .'

'Nevertheless, *Monsieur*, it is not a place one would normally choose for a gastronomic extravaganza.'

The Director made a clucking noise. 'Not all the establishments in Vichy are like the Merveilleux, Aristide.'

Monsieur Pamplemousse gave a start. In all the time he had been working for *Le Guide* it was the first occasion on which the Director had dropped so much as a hint that he might have been involved in something that had happened soon after he'd joined: a kind of initiation ceremony.

The Merveilleux had been one of his first ports of call. He'd been sent there in order to determine whether or not the hotel restaurant was suitable Stock Pot material—the award given by *Le Guide* when the *cuisine* was above average and worthy of a special visit; on a par with Michelin's *rosettes* and Gault-Millau's *toques*.

The memory of that evening had remained with him for a long time; the hush which had fallen over the other diners when he'd asked for the *à la carte menu*, only to be told there was no choice. The meal that followed was indelibly etched on his mind— *velouté de tapioca* followed by *carrottes Vichy* followed by *fruits de saison*. Clearly, from the meagre offering of the last course, it had been a bad season for fruit farmers.

Never had he eaten so many grapes at one sitting. In the end the waitress had taken the bowl away from him. And never had he felt so lonely.

Sleep had eluded him that night, as it had Pommes Frites, who was convinced he had done something wrong and was being punished; a conviction which wasn't helped through his having drunk too deeply of the local water, losing his voice as a result.

Monsieur Pamplemousse had got his own back by writing a report eulogising in great depth on his meal, fabricating a story which involved a change of ownership and a young chef destined for stardom. Another Inspector had been dispatched post haste, and from that moment on, although the Director had never referred to the matter, he had been accepted as part of the team.

'Anyway, Pamplemousse,' the Director broke into his thoughts, 'ours is not to reason why. I have to admit I asked myself the same question when I first heard of the venue. But it appears it is one of those occasions when outsiders know more about the history of a country than do its inhabitants.

'In order to find the answer one has to turn to the life and works of Alexandre Dumas. You know, of course, that he compiled one of the great culinary works of all time: *Le Grand Dictionnaire de Cuisine.*'

Monsieur Pamplemousse had to confess it was a gap in his education. 'I am aware of it, *Monsieur*, but I have never read it.'

'Ah, then you must, Aristide, you really must. It is more than a mere cookery book—it is a distillation of things learned during a whole lifetime of good eating and entertaining. It deserves to stand alongside the works of Brillat-Savarin. Sadly, it was his last work. He delivered the manuscript to his publisher, Alphonse Lemerre, in March 1870. Shortly afterwards the Franco-Prussian War broke out and publication was delayed. He died at his house just outside Dieppe while it was still at the printers.' Reaching down, the Director opened a desk drawer and removed a large, leather-bound volume. 'I will lend you my copy. I'm sure it will appeal to you.'

'*Merci, Monsieur.*' Feeling that in accepting the offer he was somehow entering into a commitment, but unable to see a way out of his predicament, Monsieur Pamplemousse reached across and took the book.

'As is so often the case,' continued the Director, 'love of food and cooking went hand in hand with the appreciation and love of other good things in life; art—he was a great friend of Monet—conversation, and, naturally, of women. One summer he took a house called the Villa André on the outskirts of Vichy in order to begin work on yet another sequel to *The Three Musketeers*. Before he started work he decided to put himself in the right frame of mind by preparing a banquet for a few close friends who were staying with him at the time. His collaborator, Auguste Maquet, was there . . . the painter Courbet . . . and Courbet's mistress, Madame de Sauvignon.

'And what a meal, Aristide. Let me read you a little of the menu.

'They began with a recipe of Dumas' own invention—*Potage à la crevette*, and for an *hors d'oeuvres* they had lampreys—cooked as they should be—in their own blood; a rare delicacy these days. *Asperge* came hard on the heels of the lampreys, followed by *ortolans* roasted on the spit.

'But the main course, the *pièce de résistance*, served after palates had been cleansed by water ices, was *Rôtie à l'Impératrice*.

'You start with an olive, remove the stone and replace it with some anchovy. Then you put the olive into a lark, the lark into a quail, the quail into a partridge, the partridge into a pheasant, the pheasant into a turkey, and then the turkey into a suckling pig. The rest is up to the chef.

'They ended the meal with peaches in red wine, pears with bacon, and *fromage*.

'Think of the ergonomics of preparing such a feast, Aristide. Imagine going into a *boucherie* or a *poissonnerie* today with such an order and asking them to ensure that every ingredient is in exactly the right state of readiness. And remember, this was long before the days of electric refrigeration.

'No doubt after such a feast the rest of the company departed to take the cure in nearby Vichy and left him in peace to write.'

'And it is that feast *Le Cercle de Six* are hoping to re-create, *Monsieur*?'

'Down to the very last detail.'

In spite of all he had said, Monsieur Pamplemousse felt himself wavering. It was an opportunity that might never occur again. Already he could see an article for *L'Escargot*—the staff magazine. Feeling a movement at his feet he glanced down and then wished he hadn't. The Director would not be pleased when he saw the state of his carpet. Pommes Frites, who had been hanging on his every word, was positively trembling with excitement. Drool issued unregarded from his mouth.

'I will see what Madame Pamplemousse has to say.' He knew exactly what Doucette would have to say when he arrived home and broke the news to her that their holiday would have to be put back. He was in for a bad evening. Lips would be pursed; sighs interspersed with recriminations. It wouldn't be the first occasion. His time in the Sûreté had been one long series of cancelled holidays.

'I will do my best, *Monsieur*. I cannot say more.'

'Good. I knew you wouldn't let me down.' The Director rose from his chair. 'Let us shake hands on it, then I will recharge our glasses so that we may drink to the venture.' For some reason he appeared to be growing agitated again; his hand, usually firm and dry, felt moist.

'You must have your photograph taken on the night, Aristide,' he called. 'Madame Pamplemousse may like one for the mantelpiece.'

Monsieur Pamplemousse contemplated the back of the Director's head. He seemed to be taking an inordinately long time over the simple task of pouring a second glass of champagne.

'May I ask, *Monsieur*, what is so special about the occasion that Madame Pamplemousse would like a photograph of me for the mantelpiece? She is well used to seeing me eat.'

Privately he felt it would be the last thing he would want to give Doucette. It would act as a constant reminder of things that might have been. It would always be 'the picture taken of Aristide enjoying himself the year we had to postpone our holiday'.

He realised the Director was speaking again.

'I was saying, Aristide, it isn't often we see you, how shall I put it?—*à travesti.*'

'*Comment, Monsieur?*' Monsieur Pamplemousse came down to earth with a bump, wondering if he had heard aright. 'Did I hear the words "fancy dress"?'

'You did, Aristide. I have given the matter a lot of thought and I think it will be singularly apposite if you go to the banquet dressed as d'Artagnan. It is not, I will freely admit, what is known in the world of the cinema as "type casting"—I would hardly describe

15

you as the athletic sort. "Dashing" is not a word which springs immediately to mind, neither is "swashbuckling". However, beggars can't be choosers.'

Monsieur Pamplemousse rose to his feet. It was the final straw. 'In that case, *Monsieur*,' he said coldly, 'I suggest you send someone else.'

'Sit down, Pamplemousse. Sit down. You make me nervous when you jump up and down like that. Mrs Van Dorman is entering into the spirit of things. She is going in costume of the period. You can hardly let France down by appearing in a lounge suit.

'Anyway, it isn't possible to send anyone else.' The Director strove hard to keep a note of irritation from his voice. 'As you are well aware, June is a busy time of the year. We drew lots yesterday morning and you came up with the short straw. Or rather, in your absence Glandier drew it for you.'

'Glandier!' Monsieur Pamplemousse stared at the Director. Things were starting to fall into place. He knew at the time it had been a mistake to take time off in order to go shopping with his wife. Shopping with Doucette was never a happy experience at the best of times; tempers were liable to become frayed. When she couldn't find the dress she wanted she had a habit of staring at the empty rack as though hoping something would materialise. That it never did and never would made no difference. All the same, it hadn't occurred to him that while he was drumming in Galeries LaFayette dark deeds were afoot.

'Have you not seen Glandier at the staff annual outing, *Monsieur*? He is the one who always brings along his conjuring outfit. He does the three-card trick better than anyone I know. He can make a *lapin* appear out of his hat as soon as look at it. They say

16

he even has a black cloth on the table when he dines at home so that he can practise in front of his wife!'

'Pamplemousse!' The Director looked mortally offended. 'You are surely not suggesting . . .'

'*Oui, Monsieur.* That is exactly what I am suggesting. I demand another draw.'

'I am sorry, Pamplemousse. That is quite out of the question. The straws have been returned to the canteen. Besides, you are the only one left. The rest of the staff have gone their separate ways.'

'As quickly as possible I would imagine,' said Monsieur Pamplemousse drily. 'You probably couldn't see them for dust.'

He ought to have known something was afoot from the smug way Glandier had said '*Bonne chance*' when they met on the stairs that morning. He'd been carrying his going-away valise as well.

Other encounters came to mind; or rather, non-encounters. Looking back on it everyone had seemed only too anxious to hurry about their business, which was unusual to say the least. Most of them were away from base so much during the year they were normally only too pleased to seize on any chance of catching up on the latest gossip.

'As part of our contribution to the event I have engaged a group of local thespians to play the part of Dumas and his guests—it will add a touch of colour. Mrs Van Dorman has expressed a wish to go as d'Artagnan's projected mistress in the new work, a certain Madame Joyeux. All in all, it promises to be an exciting evening.'

'I do not think that is a very good idea, Monsieur. It may be apposite if I go as d'Artagnan, but being accompanied by my mistress is fraught with danger.'

The Director clucked impatiently. 'Must you take

everything so literally, Pamplemousse? It will be in name only.'

'It is precisely the name, *Monsieur*, which will bother Madame Pamplemousse most. She is even more likely to take it literally than I do when I tell her.'

The Director looked startled. 'Tell her, Pamplemousse? Is that wise? Is it strictly *nécessaire?*'

'*Oui, Monsieur.*'

'But this is most unlike you. Need she ever know?'

Monsieur Pamplemousse raised his eyebrows. 'You have met Doucette, *Monsieur*. She will know. Over the years she has developed a sixth sense in such matters.'

'Mmm. Yes, I see what you mean.'

'Besides,' said Monsieur Pamplemousse virtuously. 'I have decided to turn over a new leaf. Life is too short to spend it arguing. Ever since La Rochelle . . .'

'La Rochelle?' The Director sat bolt upright and gazed at Monsieur Pamplemousse with interest. 'What happened in La Rochelle, Aristide? You did not tell me about it.'

'Nothing happened, *Monsieur.*'

'Then what are you talking about?'

'There was an unfortunate misunderstanding. Madame Pamplemousse telephoned me about something and the call was put through to my room.'

'And?'

'The chambermaid happened to pick up the receiver. She was turning the mattress at the time, and naturally she was breathing somewhat heavily.'

'I must say, Pamplemousse,' said the Director severely, 'that in view of your past reputation I would be somewhat suspicious were I your wife—which, thank

Le Bon Dieu, I am not—and I heard a young girl breathing heavily on the other end of the line.'

'She was not young, *Monsieur*. That is why she was breathing heavily. I took a photograph of her to prove my point. Unfortunately, she happened to bend over just as I pressed the shutter release and Madame Pamplemousse came across the enlargement before I had a chance to explain. The matter has come up on a number of occasions since.'

'All women nag, Aristide. They deny it, of course, but it is in their nature. Why only this morning my own dear wife informed me for the fourth or fifth time over breakfast that she never nags, and when I pointed out that repetition of certain remarks was in itself a form of nagging, all logic deserted her.'

'I am simply saying, *Monsieur*, that in view of the present atmosphere I am—how shall I say?—on trial as it were. I wouldn't wish Doucette to think I was deceiving her. Life would not be worth living. In the circumstances I shall have to tell her that I am being "accompanied" and I am not sure how she will take it.'

'So be it, Pamplemousse.' Clearly, now that he had got over the shock, the Director had filed it away in his mind as a domestic problem, and therefore no concern of his. 'If it is of any consolation, I think you will find Mrs Van Dorman is hardly one of the *grandes horizontales*. As a captain of her profession she has too many other things on her mind. Success can be very time- and energy-consuming as I know to my own cost.'

The Director managed to combine his dismissal of the problem with an airy wave of the hand which suggested he, too, had other more important matters awaiting his attention and that it was high time Monsieur Pamplemousse went on his way. For his part, Monsieur Pamplemousse was more than willing to oblige before anything else happened to disturb his peace of mind.

'Your costume will be ready on the night. Fortunately there is an opera house in Vichy, much given I am told to revivals of works of the period. Everything has been arranged. It will be delivered to your hotel two days from now. Your *cheval* will be waiting at the gates to the Villa André so that you can make your entrance.'

Monsieur Pamplemousse was in the outer office before he absorbed the full import of the Director's last words. He hesitated, wondering if he had heard aright, then knocked on the door again.

'*Entrez.*'

The Director's face fell as he caught sight of Monsieur Pamplemousse hovering in the doorway.

'You used the word *cheval*, *Monsieur*? Do you mean . . . my *deux chevaux*?'

Once again the Director had difficulty in stifling his impatience.

'No, Pamplemousse, I do *not* mean your *deux chevaux*, I mean *un cheval*. Had I meant *deux* I would have used the plural. If you are to play the part of a musketeer you must do things properly. You can hardly arrive for a nineteenth-century banquet at the wheel of a Citroën 2CV. It would be an anti-climax to say the least; somewhat akin to Cleopatra journeying down the Nile on a pedalo.'

'But, *Monsieur* . . .'

'Pamplemousse! I must say you are in a singularly difficult mood today. It is surely not asking too much of you to relinquish your car for one evening in the year. In short, to exchange your *deux chevaux* for the

20

real thing. Besides, you said yourself you are having trouble with the door. It will be a good opportunity to have it mended. Vichy is known for equestrian pursuits. It must be full of blacksmiths.'

'I shall need riding lessons, Monsieur.'

'There is no time for such luxuries, Pamplemousse!' barked the Director. 'You will hardly need lessons in order to travel the hundred metres or so up the driveway to the Villa . . . A child of five could do it blindfolded.

'In any case, I am not asking you to spring from the saddle as if you were representing France in the Olympics. Help will be near at hand.'

'But I am not insured,' protested Monsieur Pamplemousse.

The Director picked up his telephone receiver. 'I will get Madame Grante to deal with the matter immediately. She can arrange for a cover note to be issued. All it needs is a simple document. Fire and theft are hardly necessary. Third party possibly . . .'

'It is not the *third* party I am worried about, *Monsieur.*'

'Pamplemousse! I do not wish to hear another word.

'I have arranged for you to meet Mrs Van Dorman tomorrow morning at the Hôtel de Crillon where she is staying. I will accompany you to effect an introduction, then I must leave you. It so happens I have an appointment there for *déjeuner.*'

Monsieur Pamplemousse listened to the Director with a growing sense of doom, wondering if there was more to come. He hadn't long to wait for an answer.

'One last thing before you go . . .' The Director opened his desk drawer again and took out a small wicker-work container. Undoing the lid, he withdrew a graduated tumbler. 'You may as well take this. It will save buying a new one. I used it once a long time ago when I was taking the cure at Vichy. I have washed it out, but if I were you I would give it another rinse before using it. My wife finds it useful when she is spraying the roses for greenfly.'

He slid the drawer shut. 'You are fortunate to be going now. The season proper begins on 15th June, so you will miss the worst of the rush. After the 15th you can hardly get into the 'Palais des Sources' for fear of being crushed by what our American friends call *les Wrinklies*.

'*A votre santé*, Aristide. We will touch base at the Hôtel de Crillon tomorrow.'

2

FAMOUS LAST WORDS

FRESH FROM A LAST-MINUTE BRIEFING AT *LE Guide*'s headquarters off the esplanade des Invalides, Monsieur Pamplemousse crossed the Seine by the pont de l'Alma, turned right along the cours Albert 1er, negotiated the stream of traffic thundering round the place de la Concorde, and drew up outside the Hôtel de Crillon at precisely twelve noon.

As a commissionaire came forward to greet them, the Director consulted his watch. 'Good work, Pamplemousse,' he exclaimed. 'I must say . . .'

Monsieur Pamplemousse never did discover what further accolade his chief was about to bestow on him, for the sentence remained unfinished, cut off in mid-flight as it were, as its begetter suddenly vanished out of the side of the car.

The look of disbelief on the Director's face as he disappeared from view was equalled only by that of the commissionaire as he stood clutching the door of Monsieur Pamplemousse's car, unsure whether to give priority to restoring it to its rightful place or rendering assistance to the figure sprawled on the pavement at his feet.

'*Pardon, Monsieur.*' The man's normal air of aplomb deserted him as he made a fumbling attempt to hook the door back on. 'Such a thing has never happened to me before.'

'You will be hearing from my *avocat* in the morning,' said Monsieur Pamplemousse coldly. 'It may teach you to take more care in future.' He leaned across and peered out at the Director.

'I am sorry, *Monsieur*, but I did warn you. As I said in your office only yesterday, since Madame Pamplemousse had her accident, opening the door is not always easy. It is an acquired knack.'

The Director stared up at him. 'It might have become detached while we were going along!' he exclaimed. 'What then?'

'Oh, no, *Monsieur*. Once it is shut it is shut. It is when anyone tries to open it that trouble begins.'

The Director rose to his feet and dusted himself down. 'I trust it doesn't happen *en route* to Vichy. I shall never forgive myself if Mrs Van Dorman is deposited on the *autoroute*. The repercussions if she happened to be struck by a passing *camion* do not bear thinking about.'

He turned abruptly on his heels and waited by the entrance long enough for Monsieur Pamplemousse to carry out the necessary repairs, then led the way into the hotel.

'Henri!' As they entered the foyer a tall, elegant woman in her late thirties rose to greet them. Monsieur Pamplemousse caught a whiff of perfume, strong and assertive. It was not one he recognised; probably one of her own manufacture. He was aware, too, of an unexpectedly healthy tan enhancing a smile which revealed whiter than white, slightly protruding teeth. Dark sunglasses rested on a pile of blonde hair, cut to within an inch of the collar of an immaculate two-piece suit. It was not what he would have chosen for a long journey in a 2CV.

The Director was already into his 'Welcome to France' routine; an essay in Gallic gallantry. The meeting of the eyes, the slight bow, the delicate clasping of the fingertips as he raised them to his lips; the uttering of the single word *'Enchanté'* in a tone half an octave lower than normal. Mrs Van Dorman looked as though she had encountered it on previous occasions, but wasn't averse to a repeat performance.

As he was carrying out the latter part of his routine the Director gave a slight start.

'You are prepared for the journey I see.'

Monsieur Pamplemousse glanced down. In striking contrast to the rest of her outfit, Mrs Van Dorman was sporting a pair of brightly coloured designer sneakers.

'I use them when I travel. I went for an early morning jog round the Tuileries. It makes a change from Central Park. It's like I always say, a healthy body is a healthy mind.'

'I hope you are listening, Pamplemousse,' said the Director pointedly.

'Comment?' Monsieur Pamplemousse did his best to suppress a shudder as the Director introduced him to their guest. 'I am afraid my Eenglish is, 'ow do you say? a little covered in rust.'

Conscious that the Director was glaring at him across Mrs Van Dorman's shoulder, he was about to emulate the other's welcome when he thought better of it. Instead he contented himself with a brief handshake. It was reciprocated coolly but firmly. As he let go, he gave a quick glance round the foyer, half expecting to see Doucette lurking behind a potted palm. He wouldn't have put it past her. His edited version of all that had passed between himself and the Director had not gone down as well as he had hoped; the seeds of suspicion had been sown. Given the fact that Mrs. Van Dorman didn't match up in any way whatsoever with his description, the quicker they made their getaway the happier he would be. Better safe than sorry.

'I am sure you will have things to talk about with *Monsieur Le Directeur*,' he said. 'If you will allow me I will supervise the loading of the luggage.'

The Director eyed him approvingly. 'A good idea, Pamplemousse. And ... *bonne chance*. I shall await your report with interest.'

Not quite certain how to take the last remark, Monsieur Pamplemousse made his way out of the hotel to the side door in the rue Boissy d'Anglas, where the baggage of the rich and famous normally came and went.

His heart sank as he took in a pile of monogrammed valises waiting on a trolley just outside the entrance. They looked like an advertisement for a complete set of round-the-world baggage. He knew even before he saw the initials on the side whom they belonged to. Already he could see problems with Pommes Frites.

The porter's eyes said it all as Monsieur Pamplemousse led the way back into the *place* and stopped by his car. The commissionaire, his white gloves streaked with black oil, studiously turned his back on them. Monsieur Pamplemousse reached for his wallet. In a world where most things had a price he felt he could be in for an expensive time.

He became aware of the perfume again and turned to find Mrs Van Dorman standing just behind him.

'Do we have to go to all this trouble?' she asked. 'There must be an easier way. Can't we get the Car Jockey to bring the motor here, or else ask the Bell Captain to organise the porters to take the baggage straight to the car? It can't be that far away.'

'This *is* the car,' said Monsieur Pamplemousse.

Mrs Van Dorman gazed at him thoughtfully. 'You know what I thought you said?'

'*Comment?*' Monsieur Pamplemousse sought refuge in the language barrier again. 'I am afraid you will have to talk slowly. *Lentement s'il vous plaît.*'

'Oh, God!' It was hard to tell what Mrs Van Dorman might be thinking behind her dark glasses, now firmly in place over her eyes.

'As you see,' said Monsieur Pamplemousse, rolling back the canvas roof, 'the top comes away.'

'Along with the door?' The Director had obviously been recounting his experience.

'It is what we call a *deux chevaux*.'

'It looks more like a *faux pas* to me. In America we call it a roll-top desk.'

Even with the roof open, Mrs Van Dorman's luggage took up almost the whole of the back seat, rising up through the opening like a miniature Eiffel Tower. Squeezed into what little space there was left behind the passenger seat, Pommes Frites assumed one of his mournful expressions. He kept a stock of them especially for such occasions. Clearly the seating arrangements did not meet with his approval. In Pommes Frites' opinion anyone who travelled with that amount of luggage should personally suffer the consequences and not visit them on others.

They took the Porte d'Orléans exit out of Paris and then drove via the *Périphérique* on to the A6 *autoroute*. Even simple pleasantries like 'the Director is a nice man' (a statement which elicited a slightly less than enthusiastic *'oui'* from Monsieur Pamplemousse) and 'I should make sure your seat belt is tight in case the door falls off again' (greeted with even less enthusiasm by Mrs Van Dorman), which had served to break the ice while driving the length of the boulevard Raspail, dwindled away to nothing as heavy lorries roared past on either side of them. For the time being the noise of their engines drowned any further attempt at conversation.

Mrs Van Dorman, who had been growing steadily more restless as time went by, began shifting about in her seat as though she was trying to escape something unpleasant. As they stopped at the toll barrier just before entering the Forest of Fontainebleau she reached down and felt inside a black leather case at her feet.

Monsieur Pamplemousse glanced across with interest as she produced a Filofax built like a miniature desk which she spread out on her lap.

'I have a secret compartment in my right trouser leg,' he said as they moved off. 'It was made for me by Madame Pamplemousse. You will never guess what I keep in there.'

'I think I'd rather not know.'

Glancing nervously at the woods on either side, Mrs Van Dorman buried herself in an instruction booklet for a moment or two, then pressed a series of keys. A loud bleep emerged, followed by an electronic voice with Japanese overtones. Monsieur Pamplemousse made out the words 'Spume, foam, spindrift, meringue and nimbostratus'. It seemed an unlikely combination.

'Shit!' Mrs Van Dorman seemed to be expressing disappointment rather than searching for a further synonym.

'You have a problem?'

'Why is it you can look up every kind of goddamn eventuality except the one you want. If I go to the dentist and he takes out the wrong tooth I can tell him to put it back in six different languages, but ask it something simple . . .'

'What is the word you are looking for?'

'Dribble.'

'*Comment?*'

'Dribble. Your dog happens to be dribbling down the back of my neck.'

Monsieur Pamplemousse narrowly avoided careering out of his lane and into the barrier as he stole a quick glance over his shoulder. Pommes Frites, the lower part of his jaw joined to the nape of Mrs. Van Dorman's neck by a rivulet of viscous liquid, returned his gaze unblinkingly.

'*Mon Dieu!*' Monsieur Pamplemousse regained control of the car. 'It is probably the heat. In French we use the word *dégoutter.*' There were others he could think of. The phrase 'Every dog has his day' sprang to mind.

Mrs Van Dorman snapped her case shut. 'You want to know something? I'm past caring. Right? It feels the same in any language. Right?'

'*D'accord!*' Monsieur Pamplemousse felt inside his pocket.

'Would you care for a *mouchoir*—a handkerchief?' As he removed a freshly ironed square of white linen

29

from an inside pocket and unfolded it, something round and black fell out on to Mrs Van Dorman's lap. It looked like a badly squashed beetle.

'Jesus! What's that?' Only the seat belt prevented her disappearing through the open roof.

'It is a raisin—an aid to digestion. I have been reading Monsieur Dumas' *Grand Dictionnaire de Cuisine*. In it he recommends eating several large raisins after a meal. They need to be seeded, of course.'

Mrs Van Dorman greeted the news in silence.

Monsieur Pamplemousse made a mental note to stick to the main roads. He had entertained thoughts of showing his guest something of France on the way to Vichy, perhaps taking in the cathedral of Notre-Dame at Chartres, or making a detour via the hard-wood forest of Troncais which had been laid down by Louis XIV's farsighted minister, Colbert. But it was no time for history lessons. He decided to stick to the shortest route possible. Pommes Frites had a tendency to feel indisposed if he sat in the back for too long and the signs were not good.

'The book is full of interesting facts,' he continued, a note of desperation in his voice. 'Did you know, *par exemple*, that when the storks fly south for the winter and they rest for the night, the ones who are on guard duty stand on one leg in order to conceal a pebble in their other claw. Thus, if they fall asleep they will relax their grip on the pebble and the sound of it hitting the ground will cause them to wake.'

'I have to say I didn't know that.' Mrs Van Dorman gave him a strange look.

'Another interesting fact,' said Monsieur Pamplemousse, 'is that one ostrich egg is equal to ten hens' eggs.'

'I can't wait to tell my cook next time I ask her to make me an omelette.'

'There is also an interesting section on bakers and baking,' said Monsieur Pamplemousse defensively. Mentally, he was beginning to agree with Pommes Frites' summing up of the situation. Since Mrs Van Dorman was helping to organise the banquet, the least she could do was show a little interest in the subject.

His thought waves evidently struck home. 'Your English is better than you let on,' said Mrs. Van Dorman. 'Tell me about where we are going.'

'Vichy?' Glad to be on firmer ground at last, Monsieur Pamplemousse considered the question for a moment or two. 'Vichy is . . . Vichy. It is like nowhere else. You will see when you get there. To me, its one great asset is that it happens to be on the edge of the Auvergne, and the Auvergne is on the edge of another world; part of the Massif Central. Six hundred million years ago there was a cataclysmic upheaval of the ground. In consequence it is a landscape full of strange nooks and crannies. Everywhere you go you will see patches of black lava, and dotted about the countryside there are *puys*—unlikely peaks formed by the molten lava.

'People from the Auvergne are renowned for keeping their wealth under the mattress. They also bottle it. All over the area there are spas where the water gushes up out of the ground—sometimes hot, sometimes cold. Ever since Roman times people have gone there for their health; to St Nectaire for the kidneys, Royat for the heart, Le Mont-Dore for asthma and to Vichy for the digestion. There are many more besides. Each town has its speciality.

'In the spring the countryside is alive with wild

31

flowers; cowslips, celandines, snowdrops and daffodils. You open the car window as you drive along and you can smell their perfume. There are trout and salmon and crayfish in the streams and the hills are covered with yellow gorse. In summer it can be very hot. In the autumn there are crocus and spiraea.

'But I am prejudiced. It is where I was born.'

'If it's so perfect, why did you leave?'

'For the same reason as everyone else. What I have been describing is only true for part of the year. There is a price to pay for everything—especially perfection.

'The winters are cold and hard. If you live in a remote village you can be snowed up for weeks on end. There is little work. When the railways came it was hoped they would bring prosperity to the region; instead the men took advantage of it to leave home for the capital. Even the success of the spas turned against them. People began to feel that if they could buy the water at home, why bother to make the journey. Traditionally those who left became restaurateurs; they set up the first *bals musettes*; Paris became known as the biggest city in the Auvergne.'

'Have you ever thought of becoming a *restaurateur*?'

'Often. Then I go behind the scenes and I change my mind. It is also a hard life. Working for *Le Guide* I have the best of both worlds.'

They drove in silence for a while, but it was a different silence this time.

'If there is time,' said Monsieur Pamplemousse, 'I would like to take you into the mountains.'

'It makes a change from being asked to look at etchings!'

'*Comment?*'

'I'm sorry. I'm being crabby. The truth is I have bad vibes about this trip.'

'Vibes? I am sorry. I do not understand.'

'Vibrations. Feelings. Have you ever tried acting as nursemaid to six authors? Individually they're fine. But together . . . yuch!'

'Is that why you are not travelling with them? As tour leader should you not be with your troops?'

'Are you kidding? I don't mind laying on the feast; it's good publicity and we can go to town on it in the next issue. But before and after it they can look after themselves. On the surface everything is sweetness and light, but underneath it all they're as jealous as hell of each other. Do you know something? Before I left New York we had a meeting in my office. I happened to have a book written by one of them on my desk. One of the others threw it in the trash can. He made it seem like a joke, but I caught the look on his face.'

'Why do they go then?'

'Search me. I guess it's one of those things— they've been doing it for years and once you start a thing it's hard to stop. Anyway, they've all been in Annecy on some kind of mystery writers' festival. They're coming on to Vichy under their own steam.'

'Tell me about them.'

'What do you know?'

'I know only their names.' Monsieur Pamplemousse felt in a folder below his seat. The Director had given him a list that morning during the briefing.

Without taking his eyes off the road he handed a sheet of paper to Mrs Van Dorman. She scanned it briefly.

'Harvey Wentworth specialises in culinary mysteries.'

'Don't they all?'

'To a greater or lesser extent. But Harvey's hero is the only one who is actually a chef. He solves all his mysteries over a hot stove. *The Case of the Sagging Soufflé*, *Stool-pigeon Pie*, *Dinner for Two and a Half*, *Mayhem with Mustard*. His restaurant has such a high casualty rate you wonder why anyone ever goes there. He's a reviewer's delight; they can let loose with all the puns in the book. On the other hand, he knows his onions, if you'll pardon an unintentional one. He often writes for our magazine under the pseudonym of Harvey Cook.

'Then there's Harman Lock. His hero is a classical conductor who happens to be a mixture of gourmet cum detective on the side. *Schubert's Third* was all about a little old violinist called Arnold Schubert who had just one incurable weakness: little old ladies. He used to invite them up to his room to hear him play "Air on a G String", wait until they had their eyes closed, then garotte them.'

The last service area before the D7 spur beyond Nemours came and went. Monsieur Pamplemousse sensed Pommes Frites' disappointment. Pommes Frites was good on *autoroute* signs—especially those that had to do with food. He could recognise a set of crossed knives and forks a kilometre away. The car swayed slightly as he shifted his weight to look back the way they had come.

'Ed Morgan, on the other hand, writes tough gangster novels full of one-liners, with as many dead bodies to match. They have to run a shuttle service to the morgue at the end of every book while the hero goes off to lay his current girl-friend after a good homespun all-American cook-out of clam chowder followed by planked charcoal-grilled porterhouse steak, washed down by ice-cold Budweiser. His speciality is the dressing that goes with the salad. The girls can't refuse it. He has the knack of making the simple act of opening a tin of sweetcorn and stir-frying it in a saucepan sound like heaven.'

'That takes more than a knack. That takes genius. I wish I could do that.'

Mrs Van Dorman looked at him suspiciously. 'Are you taking the mickey?'

'I am being totally serious. I never knock other people's success. If I had that kind of talent it might help to sell more copies of *Le Guide*. Except the Director would never allow it.'

'When Ed Morgan writes about food, I get hungry.'

'You are hungry now?'

'I thought you'd never ask. Maybe we could pull in off the *autoroute* somewhere and grab a snack. Or get something for a picnic?'

'I'm afraid I don't have my table and chairs with me. I had to leave them out otherwise we wouldn't have got all the luggage in.'

'Do we need a table and chairs? Can't we just find a patch of grass somewhere? I could do with a good stretch.'

Monsieur Pamplemousse took the spur road. 'Only corrupt people—like the Romans and the Ancient Greeks—or those who don't care about their food lie down to eat. I know of a restaurant not far from here. It is nothing special, but for many years it has earned itself a bar stool in *Le Guide*.'

The girl at the *péage* gave Mrs Van Dorman a look of commiseration as she relieved them of 12 francs. She probably thought they were moving house on the cheap. If he'd been on his own she might well have charged commercial rates.

'Tell me about the others.' Monsieur Pample-mousse slowed down to join the N7. 'How about . . . what is the name? Monsieur Robard. I have seen his name in bookshops.'

'Paul K. Robard? Paul K. Robard has struck a rich seam in soft porn. He writes for American house-wives who work out their fantasies in the long, lonely afternoons. I'm told he's good on research too! His particular forte is recipes with sexual overtones. Five hundred unputdownable pages full of people sinking their teeth into warm, juicy peaches covered in sugar and cream, washed down with a bottle of Château d'Yquem or whatever Californian equivalent is currently available in the local supermarkets—he always makes sure he has a tie-in of some kind. The fact that the peaches may have been steeped in arsenic is beside the point. He has more fan mail than Michael Jackson. On a hot summer afternoon the bedrooms of America must be awash with scantily clad housewives drooling over their pillows.'

As they passed through Montargis Monsieur Pamplemousse found himself wondering if Mr Van Dorman had ever come home early and found his wife covered in peach juice, drooling over her pillow. It sounded unlikely—she probably worked late at the office too. Perhaps the Van Dormans were too busy ever to meet up.

Sensing from her silence he was on delicate ground, Monsieur Pamplemousse glanced across at the list. 'And Elliott Garner?'

'Elliott? He's the odd one out. He keeps himself to himself. I guess his books are more intellectual than the others; more wide ranging. He travels a lot. His hero is apt to sit on his hacienda nibbling dry biscuits over an even drier sherry. Do you know about sherry?'

Monsieur Pamplemousse shook his head.

'Then you should try reading *Bad Deeds at the Bodega*. By the time you've finished it you'll know everything there is to know, including the ins and outs of cask making . . . where the wood comes from . . . what particular part of the forest. How they bend it the way they do. He's meticulous on detail. If Elliott says something happened a certain way, you can bet your bottom dollar that's the way it was.

'This whole trip was Elliott's idea. It's his turn this year, and I'll tell you something—if nothing else it'll be well documented. Elliott's a keen photographer. And it'll go like clockwork. Not like last year when they let Spencer Troon loose and he organised a get-together in an old Death Row cell at Alcatraz.'

Monsieur Pamplemousse pondered for a moment on what a condemned man might choose to eat. 'I know what my last meal would be.'

'I wonder? I'm not sure I'd want anything—I'd be too sick with fear. The whole thing was a disaster anyway. They picked on a multiple murderer who happened to be vegetarian. Vegan at that! They had water to drink. Can you imagine?

'Spencer's high on ideas but low on research. His middle name is "Wallow". He revels in the macabre. You only have to read the list of his book titles to see the type of mind he's got: *Clinging Slime, Pus . . . Pus . . . , Death by Ordure, Worms in the Caviar . . .*' Mrs Van Dorman broke off and peered out of the window as Monsieur Pamplemousse turned off the road and parked in the last available space between a giant DAF lorry and trailer with a Dutch number plate and an even larger Mercedes from Germany.

'Is this it? The place is full of freight trucks.'

'That is because it is a *Relais Routier*. I am not

sure, but they may even have awarded it a casserole at one point.'

'You French! Stock Pots ... stars ... toques ... casseroles. You have it all tied up.'

'Life is for living,' said Monsieur Pamplemousse simply. 'Besides, to have so many *camions* outside a restaurant is a recommendation in itself.'

Mrs Van Dorman took a quick check of her appearance in the driving mirror. 'Go ahead. I'm in your hands.'

As they entered the packed restaurant there was a noticeable drop in noise level for a moment or two. Then it resumed as everyone went on with their eating.

Monsieur Pamplemousse spotted an empty table for two halfway down one wall and, after exchanging formal greetings with three men at the next table, pulled a chair out for Mrs Van Dorman.

Mrs Van Dorman looked round curiously as she sat down. 'You know something, this wouldn't happen in America.'

'You mean ... rubbing shoulders with lorry drivers? Why not? I have always thought of America as a democratic society.'

'It is, but it is also a matriarchal society and a moneyed one too. Most women who could afford it wouldn't be seen dead in a place like this.'

'Do you mind?'

'I don't mind, but if I'd known I would have dressed differently.' She gave a sniff. 'Can you smell something funny?'

Monsieur Pamplemousse glanced around him. 'It is probably a compilation; an amalgam of many smells which have permeated the woodwork over the years. *Pot au feu, navarin, café, Gauloise* ...'

'I majored in chemistry when I was at college,' said Mrs Van Dorman. 'And it isn't any of those. There's something else.'

Monsieur Pamplemousse wondered if he should point out that it might have something to do with the fact that the door leading to the toilet was just behind Mrs Van Dorman's left ear, but he forbore.

'It is perhaps nothing more than honest sweat. When you have been cooped up in a hot cab all morning . . .' He took refuge in the *carte*.

The solitary waitress slapped a basket of freshly sliced *baguette* on the table, glanced across at another table, shouted '*Commencez la tarte*' in the direction of an open hatch at the far end of the room, then stood by with a pencil poised over her pad. It boded well.

'*Vous avez choisi?*'

At a nod from Mrs Van Dorman, Monsieur Pamplemousse took charge.

He gave a quick look round the other tables and ordered the soup of the day followed by *cassoulet*.

'You know it?'

Mrs Van Dorman shook her head. 'I know of it, but I've never eaten it.'

'Ah, then you are in for a treat. From the menu I suspect the owners are from that area. We will also have a *Côtes de Rhône*.'

Monsieur Pamplemousse slapped the *carte* shut and handed it to the waitress. He would reserve judgement on the sweet until he'd seen what the others were eating. If the *tarte* were freshly made it could be good.

'They don't waste much time.'

'With only one waitress and forty *couverts* they

39

can't afford to. It is a study in time and motion, perfected over the years.'

The wine arrived in a cream and brown *pichet*, along with a *carafe* of water and a plate and bowl of water for Pommes Frites.

While they were waiting for the first course Mrs Van Dorman removed a photograph from her bag and laid it on the table.

'Take a look at what you're letting yourself in for.'

It was like all group photographs. It could have been a party of chartered accountants getting ready for their annual conference, or *Le Guide*'s staff outing in Normandy.

'They don't look as I imagined they would from the things you have already told me.'

'Who does in this world?'

That was true. Mrs Van Dorman didn't for a start. He caught a glimpse of something crisply white and taut as she leaned forward and pointed to a slight, bespectacled figure in the centre of the group.

'That's Jed Powers. And in case you're wondering why that makes seven when there are only six in the picture, it's also Ed Morgan, and if you think Ed Morgan writes toughies you should read Jed Powers. Jed Powers makes Ed Morgan read like Snow White and the Seven Dwarfs.'

'Now that *does* surprise me.'

'It surprises everyone who meets him. His real name's Norm Ellis and Norm Ellis is not only a hypochondriac with a capital H, he's frightened of his own shadow. The story goes that he passed out on the way over because he found a spider in the aircraft toilet and was in such a hurry to escape its clutches he couldn't unlock the door. It took two stewardesses and half a bottle of Scotch to bring him round. Everybody who reads his books thinks they're autobiographical, but the truth of the matter is he's so unlike his heroes his publishers daren't let him go on a promotion tour for fear of what it might do to the sales figures. He's their biggest money-spinner. He has two desks in his study and a chair on a set of rails so that he can work on the film script at the same time as he writes a book.

'Have you read *Lay Me Down to Die*?'

Monsieur Pamplemousse was forced to admit he hadn't.

'Maybe it isn't over here yet, but it will be. He's in over thirty languages. It's been on the *New York Times* Best Seller list for over six months. For a crime novel that has to be something of a record, much to the disgust of all who know him. I'm afraid our Norm is very adept at stealing other people's ideas, putting them all into the mixing-bowl he calls his head and coming out with something which he likes to think is all his own. Funnily enough, the really tough bits are. They crackle like an electric pylon in a thunderstorm.'

The soup of the day was leek and potato. Sprigs of chervil had been added and it came with croutons and a bowl of grated *Gruyère*. It was more than adequate: a meal in itself.

The *cassoulet* arrived in the pot in which it had been cooked. It was the Castelnaudary version—made without mutton or lamb, but with haricot beans, *saucisses* of the area, pork and ham. The pot was left on the table.

Monsieur Pamplemousse served two generous portions, then put some on Pommes Frites' plate; a little sausage and a portion of ham. He went easy on the beans. There was no point in asking for trouble and they still had some 250 kilometres to go.

'There is much rivalry as to which is the true version. In Carcassonne they use mutton. In Toulouse they add tomato. To be truly authentic the one we are eating should have been cooked in an oven fired with gorse from the Montagne Noire. It imparts a special flavour.'

'Tell me something. How can a nation with such abysmal taste in décor serve such wonderful food?'

Monsieur Pamplemousse looked around the room. Walls panelled with plywood in imitation matchboard; radiators with inset doors for tiny heating stoves in winter supported shelves laden with china flower-filled ducks; light fittings made of wrought iron; the patterned stone-tiled floor worn almost bare in places; pink table-cloths sporting plastic imitation straw mats; a board covered with wine labels advertising Ed. Kressman et Cie., alongside pictures of humanised dogs doing unseemly things to each other with evident enjoyment; wooden, hardbacked chairs. It was par for the course. There were thousands of places like it all over France. It wasn't the best he had ever seen, but he felt compelled to rise to its defence.

'It is a question of priorities. The food is good—that is the main thing. You might just as well ask how a nation who are able to put men on the moon and take photographs of Mars can commit so many atrocities when it comes to cooking? I have read that you cook steak in Coca-Cola.'

'You're just prejudiced. I could take you places . . . Le Cirque and Lafayette in New York. Chez Panisse in Berkeley . . .'

'So could I. You mustn't judge France by what you see here. I could take you to places where the décor and the plumbing would put anything in America to shame.'

'I bet you never put maple syrup on top of your pancakes or cinnamon on top of the coffee foam, or eat blueberry corn muffins, or put balsamic vinegar on your raspberries.' It was Mrs Van Dorman's turn to be on the defensive. 'You should try that some time. Sprinkle sugar on top and leave them to soak for two or three hours.'

'That happens to be an Italian way of doing it.'

'You French are so chauvinist. If it wasn't invented by a Frenchman it might just as well not exist.'

'We did invent the word restaurant,' said Monsieur Pamplemousse mildly. 'They came about when a certain Monsieur Boulanger began selling soups which he called "restoratives".'

While the waitress's back was turned Mrs Van Dorman surreptitiously scraped what was left on her plate into Pommes Frites' dish. 'I'm not going to make it.'

'For what it is worth, you have made a friend for life.'

'If he helps me out he'll have one too!'

Monsieur Pamplemousse wiped the inside of the tureen with the remains of his bread, toyed with the idea of ordering *tarte aux pommes*, then called for *café* and the bill instead.

'This one is on me.' Mrs Van Dorman touched the back of his hand lightly for a moment as she reached for her bag. 'I'm sorry if I'm being crabby. It's like I said earlier—I shan't rest until all this is over.'

Getting back into the car was less easily accomplished than it had been on the first occasion. Once settled, Pommes Frites closed his eyes and was soon

43

fast asleep. It wasn't long before Mrs Van Dorman did likewise.

Feeling inside the secret pocket of his right trouser leg, Monsieur Pamplemousse helped himself from a store of raisins. He chewed on it reflectively as he drove, wondering what he had let himself in for.

Halfway between Nevers and Moulins, feeling in need of some company, he turned on the radio and was just in time to catch the tail end of an item about Vichy. A man—as yet unidentified—had died while taking the waters. It must have only just happened for the details were very sketchy. No more than the bare facts. In all probability the authorities would try and play it down anyway. It wouldn't be very good publicity.

He was glad Mrs Van Dorman wasn't awake to hear it. She might have had her worst fears confirmed.

It was the middle of the evening by the time they arrived. As he tried to move his stiff and aching limbs into action, Monsieur Pamplemousse reflected they must look as though they were in Vichy for the cure, and none too soon either. Like two superannuated jockeys, they mounted the well-worn steps of the Hôtel Thermale Splendide, negotiated as best they could the vast revolving door, and checked in at the desk. Pommes Frites chose to wait outside. He mistrusted revolving doors.

Complaining that she might never walk again, let alone eat, Mrs Van Dorman said goodnight and disappeared into the lift along with her luggage and an elderly night porter with a long-suffering look on his face. Having committed his own bag to temporary safe-keeping at the desk, Monsieur Pamplemousse took Pommes Frites for a walk in the Parc des Sources by the river.

The sky was blue and cloudless; the water sparkling in the evening light. He'd forgotten how wide the Allier was at that point. Taking off from a strip of sandy beach, Pommes Frites essayed a quick dip in the river. Monsieur Pamplemousse could hardly blame him—he wouldn't have minded one himself, but given the fact that they would be sharing a room that night it wasn't the best news he'd had that day.

While he was waiting he stopped by a small riverside *café* and ordered a sandwich and a bottle of beer.

'Bad news about the death today.'

The man behind the counter gave a shrug. 'It's a wonder it doesn't happen more often when you look at some of the people who go there. Not that this one was old. Only in his forties, so they say.' He poured half the beer into a glass. 'Bet you can't guess what his last words were.'

It was the kind of question Monsieur Pamplemousse could have done without at the end of a long and tiring drive, but fortunately it was rhetorical.

'Bring me a bottle of Bâtard Montrachet and some fish.'

Monsieur Pamplemousse expressed suitable surprise.

'Now, I bet you're going to ask me "what year?" and "what sort of fish?".'

As it happened it was the last thing on Monsieur Pamplemousse's mind, but clearly he was stuck with the subject until he'd finished his snack. The man seemed glad of a new audience for a story he'd obviously repeated many times.

'He didn't specify!'

'I think,' said Monsieur Pamplemousse, 'in similar circumstances I would have tempered desire with availability. I would have settled for a bottle of

45

Muscadet and some lobster—a cold lobster, with mayonnaise and a little green salad.'

'Me, I'd have chosen a good *vin rouge* and *steak frites*.'

Several others round the bar nodded their agreement. They were about to join in when Pommes Frites, having heard his name mentioned, arrived on the scene and set about shaking himself dry.

Monsieur Pamplemousse gave him the remains of his sandwich, then beat a hasty retreat. On the way back through the old part of the town he looked for a *tabac-journaux* in the hope of buying a newspaper, but they were all closed. He toyed with the idea of searching out the house where the banquet was to take place—it was somewhere near the Pavillon Sévigné, one-time home of France's most famous letter writer, the Marquise de Sévigné—but he thought better of it. His mind was on other things. Something of Mrs Van Dorman's sense of unease had entered into him and all he really wanted to do was go to bed and get some sleep.

To his relief when he arrived back at the hotel his room was already prepared for the night; the shutters were wound down over the balcony window and the bed sheets had been turned back.

Too tired to have more than a token wash, Monsieur Pamplemousse reserved the luxury of a bath until morning and climbed straight into bed. He had hardly settled down and made himself comfortable when the telephone rang. He groped for the receiver.

'Aristide?'

It was Mrs Van Dorman. She was one up on him. He had no idea what her Christian name might be.

'*Oui.*'

'It's DiAnn . . . Can I ask you something?'

'Of course.' He wondered what was coming.

'Do you think it's safe to drink the water?'

It wasn't until he had put the phone down and turned out the light once again that the irony of the question struck him. It was a good job Mrs Van Dorman had asked him and not the night porter. The latter might well have taken umbrage.

On the other hand . . . he closed his eyes, allowing himself the luxury of drifting to sleep on thoughts which floated in and out of his mind like the waves of an incoming tide . . . on the other hand, there was one person in Vichy who might well have had a different answer had he still been alive to voice it.

3

TROUBLED WATERS

MONSIEUR PAMPLEMOUSSE WOKE TO THE SOUND of a road-cleaning machine making its early morning rounds outside the hotel. If the noise was anything to go by, the driver was a strong union man. One up the lot up.

Pommes Frites opened one jaundiced eye and, when he saw the room was still in semi-darkness, closed it again. Monsieur Pamplemousse tried following suit for a while, but he had too much on his mind to go back to sleep and in the end he got out of bed and wound open the shutter covering the balcony window. Then he opened the door and went outside.

The road below was still gleaming where it had been freshly sprayed with water; the locals must be expecting the early summer they had been enjoying to stay for a while. The temperature in Paris had been in the upper seventies; today looked as though it might be even hotter. Looking eastwards over the rooftops he could barely make out the foothills of the Monts de la Madeleine, some twenty kilometres away, for the intervening countryside was shrouded in a heat haze.

Monsieur Pamplemousse looked at his watch. It was already nine o'clock. He hadn't slept so late in years.

While he was shaving he ran the bath. It was a giant of a thing, with taps and pipework to match; the product of a bygone age. Undoubtedly it would confirm Mrs Van Dorman's worst suspicions about French plumbing. On the other hand, she couldn't have grumbled about the water. It was what his old mother would have called 'piping hot'. In its heyday the hotel must have needed a boiler the size of an ocean liner's. At least it still worked, which was more than could be said for the row of bell-pushes alongside the bed; one marked *Femme de Chambre*, another *Valet de Chambre* and a third *Sommelier*. At some point in time the wires had been severed at the skirting board, the paint-covered ends still protruded from beneath the well-worn patterned carpet. As he lay back in the bath, Monsieur Pamplemousse reflected on how nice it must have been to stay in bed of a morning and summon help from all directions when you felt like it, instead of having to hang a breakfast order on a door knob outside the room the night before.

One came across such places from time to time, mostly in old spa towns or once fashionable seaside resorts. Dinosaurs of the hotel trade, they were mostly staffed by old retainers who had nowhere else to go, and when they died the hotel would die too.

Hearing the sound of splashing, Pommes Frites

came into the room and rested his chin on the side of
the bath. Even he looked a little taken aback by its
size. Monsieur Pamplemousse hoped it wouldn't occur to him that there was room for them both, or
even essay an attempt to rescue his master.

He was saved by a knock on the outer door, re-
minding him that he'd ordered his breakfast for nine-
fifteen.

'*Entrez!*' Reaching for the flannel, he sank down
into the water.

The chambermaid was unperturbed. '*Sur le balcon,
Monsieur?*' She didn't give him time to reply as she
bustled past the open bathroom door carrying a tray.
There was a rattle of crockery from somewhere out-
side and the sound of chairs being moved, then a
'*Bon, appétit, Monsieur,*' and she was gone again.

She was right, of course. It was no morning for sitting in one's room eating *croissants* by electric light.

Swathed in a voluminous towelling dressing-gown,
courtesy of the hotel, Monsieur Pamplemousse found
the town plan the Director had provided him with,
then went out on to the balcony and poured himself
a cup of *café*.

He gazed across the town. Apart from a few desultory figures taking the air, the Parc des Sources was
deserted. Dozens of white, wrought-iron chairs were
scattered in small groups along the crisscrossing
paths as though waiting for something to happen,
their filigree backs casting photogenic shadows from
the morning sun. Two workmen in blue overalls were
busy attending to the steps in front of the Opera
House, their besoms making long arcing motions as
they swept all before them with the practised ease of
those who performed the same task day in day out all
through the year. A large billboard advertised a pro-

gramme of opera music, but it was at too much of an angle for him to read the small print. A miniature white train appeared out of a side turning, crossed the street into the park and drew up on a path near the bandstand to await the first load of tourists for the day.

Monsieur Pamplemousse decided that if he had any time to spare he might load up his camera and set out on a voyage of exploration later in the day.

Vichy looked as though it had changed very little since his last visit; or even since he had been there as a small child. In those days it had been an annual treat, but that was before its name had gone down in history as the seat of wartime capitulation. He doubted if his parents had ever gone there again, such was their shame. The centre of the town was uniquely pre-war. Seedy in places, but still with a certain dignity.

True, it now had its modern side—the area by the river—the *Bassin International D'Aviron-Voile-Motonautisme-Ski* as it was grandly marked on the map; but the old part, the arcaded walks around the park, the antique shops, the kiosks selling 'Vichy Pastilles' and the facilities for 'taking the cure' were still there. Before the war visits to the spa had been the prerogative of the rich and well to do. Now it was mostly on the National Health.

He sat up and concentrated his attention on the far side of the park as a familiar figure came into view. It was Mrs Van Dorman, weaving her way in and out of the chairs as she returned from a jog.

She was wearing a dark blue towelling track suit, with a matching blue sweat-band round her forehead. She looked undeniably healthy. Healthy and chic. Central Park's loss was undoubtedly Vichy's

51

gain. She was keeping up a fast pace—running rather than jogging. He wondered idly how she would look without her suit. In shorts perhaps? Would bare muscles ripple in the morning sun? It was one of life's little mysteries which would probably never be revealed.

Fancy asking if it was safe to drink the water! He couldn't wait to tell his colleagues back in the office. If it had been anyone else he might have suspected an ulterior motive behind the call, but as it was he felt on safe ground.

As Mrs Van Dorman drew near, Monsieur Pamplemousse saw she was carrying a tiny plaited straw case by its handle. It was similar in size to the one the Director had given him—*de rigueur* for anyone 'taking the cure'. Six times a day the Parc des Sources would be full of people carrying identical cases as they made their way to and fro between their hotel and the Hall at the far end. In between times the park would be almost empty again. Perhaps Mrs Van Dorman had bought a drinking glass as a souvenir for her husband, or she might even have decided to take the waters herself.

As she crossed the road and disappeared from view somewhere below him, Monsieur Pamplemousse turned back into his room. Seeing him go, a waiting sparrow fluttered down on to the table. Keeping one beady eye on Pommes Frites, it lost no time in pecking up the crumbs. Pommes Frites, for his part, eyed the bird with the air of one who couldn't be bothered with such trifles.

The maid had left a copy of *La Montagne* on a table in the room. Monsieur Pamplemousse picked it up and glanced at the headlines. Sport and agriculture seemed to be the dominant topics. It wasn't until he reached the back page that he came across the item

52

he was looking for. It was under the headline VICHY TRAGÉDIE—LE MYSTÈRE. There followed a noncommittal statement from the local police to the effect that they were pursuing their inquiries, but it told him nothing new; rather less in fact, for there was no mention of the man's last request. Perhaps that bit of it was a joke on someone's part. It did sound highly unlikely. The whole thing was a journalistic exercise in filling up the maximum amount of space with the minimum number of facts. By tomorrow it probably wouldn't even get a mention.

Remembering that in his haste to have breakfast he hadn't emptied the bath Monsieur Pamplemousse went into the other room and turned a large wheel between the two taps. The water made an interesting noise as it ran away; a series of rhythmic bangs and thumps reminiscent of a blacksmith hard at work.

It was only after the last of the water had disappeared with an extra loud 'glug' that he realised the knocking was being augmented by someone outside. Cursing the maid under his breath for not leaving him in peace—she probably wanted the tray back so that she could get away early—he went into the bedroom and opened the door.

To his surprise it was Mrs Van Dorman. Her face was devoid of make-up and he realised for the first time how blue her eyes were; they matched her track suit. Holding the door open he was also very aware of the warmth from her body as she squeezed past him.

'Have you heard the news?'

'Tell me.'

'That man who died yesterday. The one in the spa. It was Norm Ellis.'

'Norm Ellis? *Morbleu!*' No wonder Mrs Van Dorman had been in a hurry. 'Is he not the short one

53

with glasses who writes under several different names?'

'Right . . . Ed Morgan . . . Jed Powers and others he was trying hard to forget. Apparently he was tasting the waters in the Parc des Sources yesterday afternoon when he collapsed in a heap. It was all over before anyone could do anything. They called for an ambulance, but by the time it arrived he was dead.' Mrs Van Dorman swallowed hard. 'You're not going to believe the next bit.'

Monsieur Pamplemousse couldn't resist it. 'Before he died he asked for a bottle of Bâtard Montrachet and some fish.'

Mrs Van Dorman stared at him. 'How did you know that?'

'No matter. What I didn't know was that it was Monsieur Ellis. There was no mention of it in the *journal*.'

'But do you know something even stranger? According to the others Norm Ellis not only doesn't know one wine from another, but if you gave him a bottle and a corkscrew he wouldn't know which end to open without looking up the instructions. Budweiser is more his line.'

'*Extraordinaire!*'

'Is that all you can say? We're talking about Norm Ellis. The same Norm Ellis who's been on the bestseller lists for over six months. Someone's going to have to break the news to his publishers, and you know who that's going to be.'

'How about his wife?'

'He doesn't have a wife. He lives with his mother.'

'His mother, then.'

'I guess you're right. I'd better phone his agent.' Mrs Van Dorman looked at her watch. 'Anyway, I can leave it for a while. It'll be three o'clock in the morning there. I'm sorry . . .' she perched herself on the edge of the bed, 'but I still can't believe it. I feel responsible in a way. If only I'd been here earlier.'

'Death comes to us all in the end,' said Monsieur Pamplemousse. 'Even to those who spend their life writing about it.' It sounded too sanctimonious for words, but it was all he could think of on the spur of the moment.

'But Norm of all people. He never goes outside the door without a medical. What a way to go—in a French spa!'

'Are you certain it was him?'

'It's Norm all right. It has to be. He checked in at his hotel yesterday lunchtime along with the others. Then he said he was off to take the waters and explore the town, so he might not be back until late. They all agreed to meet up for an early breakfast. It was only when he didn't put in an appearance that they started to get worried. When they checked his room they found the bed hadn't been slept in. All the others are convinced it's him. Spencer Troon is off to identify the body. Trust him. Offer Spencer a trip to the morgue and he's there like a shot.'

'You have seen the others already?' Monsieur Pamplemousse began to wish he'd asked for an early morning call. Everyone else seemed to have been up for hours.

'They're staying just down the road from here. I called in to see how they were doing. That's how I found out about Norm. They'd been trying to phone me.'

'How are they taking it?'

Mrs Van Dorman shrugged. 'OK, I guess. It's hard to say. It doesn't seem to have hit them yet. Harvey had gone back to his room by the time I got there, and Elliott was already round at the Villa André. It hasn't put the rest of them off their breakfast, that's for sure. They were tucking in like there was no tomorrow when I saw them. You know what Harman Lock said?'

Monsieur Pamplemousse shook his head. It was too early for guessing games.

' "Trust Norm to pull a fast one!" Anyone would think he'd done it on purpose.'

She held up the case she'd been carrying. 'Do you realise that's all we have left of him—apart from his luggage! Jesus—that's another thing. I guess I'll have to do something about that.'

Monsieur Pamplemousse stared at the case. 'You mean that was his? Where did you get it?'

'One of the attendants at the spa gave it to me. As soon as I said I was a personal friend she went to a cupboard and fished it out. They came across it yesterday after he had been taken away. Apparently some little old lady went off with it to see if she could get some wine for him and by the time she got back Norm had been taken away, so she handed it in.'

'May I see it?'

She hesitated for a moment before passing him the case. 'I guess maybe I ought to hand it over to the police, although it's hardly "exhibit A".'

Monsieur Pamplemousse turned it over in his hand. The initials N. E. were stamped on the leather fastener. Further proof of the identity of the corpse, if proof were needed.

'Would you like me to see them? I may be able to find out more.'

'Would you? That'd be great. If I go there could be a communication problem. There's just so far you can get with sign language. Besides, I've got so much to do today what with the banquet and now this.'

'You are still going ahead with it?'

'I guess so. It would be crazy not to after all the work that's gone into it. I tell myself Norm would have wanted it that way. Maybe he had it on his mind when he collapsed—that's why he said what he did.'

'Where will I see you?'

'I shall be at the Villa André most of the time. I have to make sure they have all the food and that the chefs are happy ... then I have to go for a costume fitting.' She paused at the door. 'Is what the Director told me true—you're going as d'Artagnan?'

Monsieur Pamplemousse nodded dolefully. He had almost forgotten about that side of the affair.

'And I am your mistress?'

'That also is true.'

Mrs Van Dorman gave a giggle. 'I was reading up about Alexandre Dumas last night. His last affair was with a stage horseback rider called Adah Menkin. He was sixty-five at the time would you believe?'

'It is no age,' said Monsieur Pamplemousse firmly. 'Dumas had a reputation for being very active in all his pursuits. They say in many respects he had the strength of ten men.'

'I can't wait.'

While he finished dressing, Monsieur Pamplemousse began exploring the room, pondering over Mrs Van Dorman's last remark as he did so. There was a row of books on a shelf let into one of the alcoves: *Memoires de Guerre* by someone called Lloyd George; Simenon's *Le Testament Donadieu*, and a set of encyclopaedias.

A picture of a sailing ship caught in a storm at sea adorned the wall above the huge brass bedstead.

The built-in wardrobe was vast—like another small room. On the inside of the door there was a yellowing inventory of fixtures and fittings. It read like a wedding list and was comprehensive enough to have furnished many a small household.

The only concessions to modernity were a remotely controlled television standing in a corner near the balcony and a large refrigerator which he came across in yet another cupboard. It accounted for the faint hum he'd heard during the night. Hoping it might be stocked with goodies, he opened the door. It was completely bare.

He tried out the television. It was a children's panel game. He was about to switch channels when the phone rang. It was the Director. With the briefest of *bonjours* he waded straight in.

'This is bad news, Pamplemousse.'

Unsure as to exactly how much the Director knew, Monsieur Pamplemousse essayed a non-committal *'Oui, Monsieur'* in reply.

'I heard about the death on television yesterday evening, but I had no idea it was one of Madame Van Dorman's party.' Already the Director was distancing himself from the affair.

'It is very sad, *Monsieur*. I gather he was only in his early forties. It is no age.'

'Yes, of course. *Très triste. Très triste.*' There followed a short, but nicely judged pause of respect for the departed during which Monsieur Pamplemousse could almost feel the appropriate number of seconds being counted off. 'However, I was really thinking of how it might affect *Le Guide*. I have already taken the precaution of speaking to an old friend of mine—a Deputy. We were at school together. He has promised to do his best to hush matters up. You know what the *journaux* are like when they get a sniff of something.'

'You have been told what his last words were, *Monsieur*?'

'*Extraordinaire*, Pamplemousse, do you not think? And why a Bâtard Montrachet. Why not a Montrachet itself. That would have had the twin merits of being less of a mouthful to say and being a marginally better wine.'

'May I ask how you got to know, *Monsieur*?'

'You may well indeed. I was woken in the early hours of this morning by a telephone call from the police. It seems that for some strange reason the man's pockets were devoid of anything which might provide a clue as to his identity. The only thing the police could find was the address of *Le Guide* written on a scrap of paper. The night staff at the office put them through to me. I managed to stall on the true reason for his being in Vichy, and in particular our own association with the event . . .'

'But surely, *Monsieur*, it is not the end of the world. By the law of averages such things must happen in a spa from time to time. It is unfortunate he was one of our party, but I fail to see how it could reflect badly on us. There is nothing sinister about it. People die every day.'

'Be that as it may, Pamplemousse, it is the kind of thing a reporter might make capital of, particularly if jogged into action by one of our rivals. That is why I am saying we must exercise extreme caution. I am relying on you to keep a watchful eye on things at your end to make sure they don't get out of hand.

'The fact of the matter is we have an ongoing situation with Mrs Van Dorman. It is a meaningful relationship, and one which I hope will enable us to maximise our potential in the years to come . . .'

Monsieur Pamplemousse listened to his chief with only half an ear. The Director was wearing his new hat again—the one he had brought back from Bloomingdales on Lexington Avenue. Cupping the receiver between his head and his shoulder, Monsieur Pamplemousse idly opened the case Mrs Van Dorman had given him and removed the drinking glass. His first reaction was that it was almost identical to his own. They probably all came like it. He had used the one the Director had given him for a glass of water when he went to bed. Picking it up he compared the two. They both had the same gradations on the side— from 0 to 150. He raised the second glass up to the light. It was clean apart from some kind of clear deposit round the inside near the bottom. He held it to his nose. He could still detect the characteristic volcanic sulphury smell of the waters; that, and potassium nitrate, but underlying it there was something else again which he couldn't quite place.

Seeing Pommes Frites watching his every movement he held it out for him to examine. Using his large ears as a shield, Pommes Frites applied the smell receptors at the tip of his nose to the opening, sniffed deeply, then committed the result to that section of his olfactory system which contained his comparison charts. After a moment's hesitation while wheels turned and mental card indexes were consulted in order to form an evaluation, his face took on a thoughtful expression.

'Are you there?' A petulant voice in Monsieur Pamplemousse's left ear brought him back to earth.

'*Oui, Monsieur.*'

'I was saying, it is too late now to go back on our

undertaking to Mrs Van Dorman—the die is cast—but it is not a good start. I suggest you play down our involvement. Above all, Pamplemousse, keep a low profile; merge into the background as much as you can.'

Monsieur Pamplemousse contemplated the end of the telephone receiver for a moment or two while he counted up to *dix*. It was sometimes hard to come to terms with the Director's conflicting demands. On the one hand the constant desire for publicity, on the other a fear of it back-firing.

'With respect, *Monsieur*, it will be a little difficult to merge into the background if I am to attend tonight's banquet dressed as a character from *Les Trois Mousquetaires*.'

'Pamplemousse, whenever you begin a sentence using the phrase "with respect", I know full well you are about to be difficult. All I ask is that you behave as d'Artagnan would have done. No more, no less. If I remember correctly, he was constantly merging. What was the phrase? "They seek him here, they seek him there" . . .'

'I think *Monsieur* is mixing him up with the Scarlet Pimpernel. In any case he had the advantage of being dressed as others were at that period in time. I shall not be. Also, he did not have to drive through Vichy in a *deux chevaux*.'

'Then don't do it, Pamplemousse. Go by some other means.'

'Very good, *Monsieur*. I will hire a taxi. I am sure that in the circumstances Madame Grante will agree to the added expense. Or perhaps if it is a fine evening I might even arrange to have the horse delivered to my hotel instead of having it wait for me at the Villa André. No doubt the town will be full of others doing the same thing.'

There was a pause and when the Director spoke again it was in tones of resignation.

'Aristide, I am not a superstitious person, but I have to tell you the air in Paris is rife with ill omens. Last night I was kept awake for several hours by the sound of a screeching barn owl outside my window. As if that wasn't bad enough, this morning as I was about to enter the office building I walked under a ladder. Naturally I immediately retraced my steps in order to spit through its rungs three times, and in so doing I inadvertently stepped in a large pot of paint.'

The Director paused. 'I will leave you to guess what happened next.'

Monsieur Pamplemousse hesitated. It was hardly possible there could be more, but luckily the Director didn't expect an answer.

'When I carried out my intention of spitting through the rungs in order to counteract the ill luck brought on by walking under the ladder in the first place, my *salive* landed on a black cat which happened to be passing behind it at the time. Furthermore, Aristide, the animal was crossing my path in the worst possible direction—from left to right. It was not amused.

'One might argue that if a *chat*, whatever its colour, chooses to walk under a ladder, then it, too, is tempting fate and must expect to suffer the consequences. However, I cannot help thinking that someone, somewhere is trying to tell me something. That is all.' There was a click and the line went dead.

Monsieur Pamplemousse replaced his own receiver. He could see now why the Director wasn't bubbling over with happiness. Crossing to the balcony, he looked out across the red-tiled rooftops of the town while he adjusted his tie. The background mist had lifted and he could now see the countryside clearly. Below him the park was suddenly full of people; blue and white parasols adorned the tables. The sweepers had finished their work and were in consultation with each other over what to do next.

It would be very easy to laugh off the Director's fears, but on the other hand he had to admit the whole thing was really rather odd.

For a start it was strange that Norm Ellis should have nothing on him in the way of identification. In his own experience almost everyone—unless they happened to be completely down and out—carried something about their person; a diary, a wallet containing odd items, credit cards. He could hardly have been robbed. By the sound of it there had been too many people around. Perhaps, for some reason best known to himself, Norm hadn't wanted to be identified. But if not, why not? He wished now he'd thought to ask Mrs Van Dorman if any of those things had been found in his hotel.

Monsieur Pamplemousse went back into his room and picked up the tumblers again, holding them up to the light and comparing the two. Apart from the slight roughness which he'd noticed earlier in the bottom of the one used by Norm Ellis, they both looked identical. Someone, somewhere, must turn them out in their thousands. Wetting his index finger, he reached down inside the second glass and just managed to press it against the deposit. It felt slightly sticky to the touch.

Resisting the temptation to taste it, Monsieur Pamplemousse hesitated for a moment, then picked up the phone and dialled the code for an outside line, followed by his office number.

'Operations?

'Pamplemousse here.

'Oh, *ça va, ça va*. Tell me, do you have Glandier's number?

'*Merci. Au revoir.*'

Glandier was roughing it in Reims. No doubt preparing himself for a visit to Boyer to check on its three Stock Pots.

Dialling the number he had been given, Monsieur Pamplemousse struck lucky. Glandier was about to set off on his travels.

'How are things in Vichy?'

'Oh, *ça va, ça va*. Tell me about trick glasses; the sort magicians use.'

'What do you want to know?'

'Can anyone buy them?'

'It depends how sophisticated you want them to be. If you mean the drinking beer out of a tankard type—the sort where a small amount of liquid is contained inside a double skin between the inner and the outer glass—you can buy those in any good magic shop, or even in one of those joke shops. You know—the kind of place that sells "whoopee cushions" or plastic dog's *merde*, blood capsules—that kind of thing.'

'How about a tasting glass? The sort they would have at a spa?'

'A tasting glass?' Glandier pondered the question for a moment. 'I haven't ever come across one. You can get wine glasses. You've probably seen them. They look as though they're full of wine, but when you hold them upside down nothing comes out. You would need to go to someone who specialises . . . I could give you the name of a firm in Paris. In New York there's a shop on West 34th Street called "The Magic Center". I've sent away there for things myself from time to time. That sort of place is usually run by an ex-pro., so if you want something really special they always know people who will make it for you—at a price.'

'How about other kinds of tricks?' He tried a long shot. 'Water into wine for example.'

'That's usually a case of the quickness of the hand deceiving the eye. Plus a few chemicals. Take a jug of water mixed with ten per cent sulphuric acid, pour it into a glass containing a pinch of potassium permanganate and hey presto! you have a glass of red wine. Only get rid of it quickly before anyone has a chance to sample the result.'

'Hey! Don't tell me you're taking up conjuring too?'

Avoiding the question, Monsieur Pamplemousse thanked Glandier and hung up. He sensed the other's interest being roused. Another moment and he would be offering advice on how to saw Mrs Van Dorman in two.

As he replaced the receiver Pommes Frites stood up, wagging his tail. Monsieur Pamplemousse took the hint. Clearly, fifty per cent of the room's occupants thought it was high time they went for a walk.

He wondered whether he ought to contact the police as he'd promised. But that was before he'd spoken to the Director. No doubt if he rang an ex-colleague in Paris he would be given a name, but that would mean explaining why he was there and even if they were being 'leant on' from on high by a Deputy, the chances were that someone might pass on the news if only out of pique.

The phone rang. It was Mrs Van Dorman.

'I've been thinking. There's no reason on earth why you should be saddled with my problems. If you'd like to drop Norm's glass back I'll take it in to the police on my way to the Villa André.'

'It is no trouble . . .'

'No, really. It'll be a good test of my French. Besides, they're bound to ask questions you may not be able to answer. I'm about to have a bath but the maid is doing the room so you can leave it with her.'

Feeling somewhat deflated, Monsieur Pamplemousse sat on the edge of his bed for a moment or two lost in thought. Then, acting on an impulse he would have been hard put to explain, let alone justify, he swopped the two glasses over. If anyone queried it he could always plead a mistake on his part. Whether or not he would be believed was immaterial.

The room maid was busy with a feather duster. He watched while she put the case on Mrs Van Dorman's dressing table. The sound of running water came from the bathroom.

'My room is free if you wish to clean it.' He preempted the question he knew she was about to ask.

Strolling through the old town, Monsieur Pamplemousse tried to get himself in the mood for the evening's event, picturing what it must have been like in Dumas' time. The whole history of the writing of *Les Trois Mousquetaires*: the fact that the characters of Athos, Porthos and Aramis—even that of d'Artagnan—were based on real people, made fascinating reading. Dumas had certainly done well out of it, as he had from *The Count of Monte Cristo*. Long queues had formed in Paris whenever a new episode was due, and outside the capital crowds gathered to greet the arrival of the stage coach carrying copies of those *journaux* serialising the story.

By the time Dumas arrived in Vichy to begin work on yet another sequel his fame as a gourmand and *bon viveur*, as well as a womaniser, must have gone before him. At the height of his success, with over

400 literary works to his credit, he had built a mansion outside Paris—the Château Monte Cristo—to accommodate his many guests, and then he'd had to build another small house alongside—the Château d'If—as a retreat where he could escape from it all in order to work! The penalties of fame!

Having explored the town to his satisfaction, Monsieur Pamplemousse took a short cut down the rue du Docteur Fouet (*Superintendent des Eaux Minérales de Vichy*—1646–1715)—an achievement commemorated some three centuries later by Pommes Frites who paused at the corner to leave his mark, and together they made their way towards the Villa André.

Nothing in Monsieur Pamplemousse's musings had prepared him for what he found. After the sunshine the house felt darker than it probably was, but clearly, he was witnessing a no-expense-spared operation. The Villa André, which by all accounts had remained empty for some years, had undergone a transformation. It was hard to tell whether the heavy oak furniture had been brought in specially for the occasion or if it had been there all the time, but as he picked his way in and out of the rooms it felt like the opening night of some theatrical extravaganza. Girls were busy dusting and polishing chairs and tables which looked as though they could well have been there when Dumas was staying; others were cleaning silver.

In the kitchen someone—from the Nikon slung round his neck at the ready he guessed it must be Elliott Garner—was engaged in a technical argument with the *chef-de-cuisine* over the method of serving. According to Elliott the dinner had taken place on Friday 23rd June 1862, eight years before Dumas died.

The problem centred over whether the serving should be *à la Française*, as it would have been up until about 1860, when all the dishes were brought in and presented at table before being taken away to be carved, or *à la Russe*—introduced soon after that date—in which the carving was done in advance and brought in to be eaten straight away.

It was hard to tell who was winning, but Elliott Garner was obviously taking it to heart and looked as though he was ahead on points. It struck Monsieur Pamplemousse as being a little late in the day.

The *Rôtisseur* was keeping his thoughts to himself as he tackled the daunting task of preparing the *pièce de résistance*—the *Rôtie à l'Impératrice*. If it was only half as complex as the Director had described it, he would be occupied for the whole of the morning.

Monsieur Pamplemousse drifted away to explore the rest of the house. No stone seemed to have been left unturned, no expense spared to ensure the evening's success. In the dining-room silver candelabra graced a huge table laid for twelve. He arrived just as a waiter was about to remove one of the place settings.

One thing was for sure, if the number of glasses was anything to go by Norm Ellis would have made up for lost time in his consumption of wine. He might even have got to taste the Bâtard Montrachet he'd hankered after.

He bumped into Mrs Van Dorman in the corridor outside. She was dressed in white overalls.

'Am I glad to see you!'

Monsieur Pamplemousse looked suitably gratified.

'Do you feel like an *apéritif*?'

'If an *apéritif* means what I think it means—an appetiser before lunch—then the answer is "no". I'm

saving myself for tonight. But I could use a drink.'
Mrs Van Dorman looked at her watch. 'Anyway, it's
time I went back to the hotel. I have a fitting for my
dress at twelve-thirty. Maybe we could have a quick
one there.'

'Since we are about to enter into the mood of
d'Artagnan, why not a *Pousse Rapière*—a "rapier
thrust", or even a *Badinquet*?'

'Tell me?'

'The first is made from Armagnac and sparkling
white wine—ideally a *vin sauvage* from the region of
Gers, garnished with orange peel. For the second a
teaspoon of *Crème de Cassis* is mixed in with the Armagnac and a still white champagne is used.'

The barman at the hotel professed never to have
heard of either. It was said in the tone of voice imply-
ing that if *he* didn't know about it then it didn't exist.
Monsieur Pamplemousse settled for two Kirs. It
wasn't worth an argument. Once again he found
himself apologising.

'I know the type. He is like the people from Bordeaux who pretend they have never heard of Burgundy, and vice versa. The drinks I mentioned come
from the Pyrénées and to him they don't exist.'

He looked at Mrs Van Dorman as she sipped her
Kir reflectively.

'Is anything the matter? You look worried.' It was a
stupid question. She must have a lot on her mind.

'You know it definitely is—or was—Norm. Spencer
confirmed it when he got back from the morgue. He
looked like he'd seen a ghost.'

'Was there any doubt?'

'I didn't think so, but the others did apparently. Either that or it's only just hit them. I was there when
Spencer broke the news. You could have knocked any

of them down with a feather. All except Elliott, and he was too busy arguing with the chef. Harman Lock was all for calling the whole thing off. *And* there's going to be an autopsy.'

'That is normal when someone dies away from home.'

'All the same, I shall feel happier when tonight's over.' Mrs Van Dorman finished off her drink. 'Talking of which, it's time I got ready for my fitting.'

'I, too, have a fitting,' said Monsieur Pamplemousse gloomily. 'I am not looking forward to it.'

He paid the bill and having collected the keys at the desk they went up in the lift together, each lost in their own thoughts.

'See you!' Mrs Van Dorman paused at her door. 'Good luck.'

'*À bientôt.*'

Further along the corridor, Monsieur Pamplemousse turned a corner, unlocked his own door, and was in the act of removing his jacket when the telephone rang.

'Aristide—can you come quickly.' It was Mrs Van Dorman. She sounded distraught.

'Of course. I will be right with you.'

With Pommes Frites hard on his heels Monsieur Pamplemousse retraced his steps as fast as he could go. He found Mrs Van Dorman waiting for him just inside her room. She looked flushed, as well she might.

'*Merde!*' Monsieur Pamplemousse took in the scene. It was familiar to anyone who had spent time in the police; drawers half open, clothes scattered, suitcases upended. Whoever had done it had been in a hurry.

'Did you leave anything of value?'

Mrs Van Dorman shook her head. 'I had all my money and travellers' cheques with me. My jewellery is in the hotel safe.'

'Passport?'

'That's OK too. It was in my handbag.'

Monsieur Pamplemousse crossed to the balcony and tried the French windows. They were locked from the inside.

'And the main door was locked?'

Mrs Van Dorman nodded. 'I remember trying it when I left this morning. And it was certainly still locked when I came back in just now.'

'Then whoever did it must have had a key.'

'It certainly wasn't mine. You saw me pick it up from the desk.'

Monsieur Pamplemousse shrugged. 'Someone may have "borrowed" it on a pretext. In a hotel this size they would stand a good chance of getting away with it. It might even have been someone who's stayed here before and "lost" the key. It wouldn't be the first time that's happened. There are a dozen ways.'

'You don't think it could be one of the staff?'

'I doubt it. They wouldn't have made such a mess. Have you reported it yet?'

'No, I rang you first.' While they were talking Mrs Van Dorman went through her belongings. 'Anyway, nothing seems to be missing. Unless . . .' she paused by the dressing table. 'That's strange. I can't see Norm's glass anywhere.'

'You mean you hadn't taken it to the police.'

'No. In the end I was running late, so I thought I'd do it this afternoon. What do you think it means?'

Monsieur Pamplemousse gave a non-committal grunt, but behind it his mind was racing.

Mrs Van Dorman reached for the phone. 'I guess I'd better call the desk.'

While she was talking, Monsieur Pamplemousse took a last look round the room—under the bed, in the bathroom, and finally in the wardrobe.

'If you like I will leave Pommes Frites with you.'

'I'll be all right once the mess is cleared up. Besides, the costumier should be here any moment.'

'Well, you know where I am. You only have to call.'

'Thanks.' Mrs Van Dorman reached out and gave his hand a squeeze. 'I'm beginning to wonder what I'd do without you.'

Back in his own room, Monsieur Pamplemousse prowled around for a while lost in thought. He wasn't normally superstitious, but he was beginning to think that perhaps the Director was right in his fears. Come to think of it, on the journey down even Mrs Van Dorman had admitted to having "bad vibes".

For want of something better to do he picked up the case containing Ellis's glass and opened it. Removing the glass, he tried sniffing it again, this time warming the outside with his hands first to release the vapour, then emulating Pommes Frites by forming them into a screen so that the smell would be trapped. Ignoring the prickle in his nose and at the back of his throat from the sulphur and the very definite odour of potassium nitrate, he concentrated on the third smell. As with a wine, it needed only a moment—anything longer was a waste of time. First impressions were the most reliable. He tried again and this time it came to him—a very faint trace of almonds; the kind of smell which in its bitter form indicated a badly fined wine. The Germans had a good word for it—*mandelbitter*.

Mandelbitter, or . . . Monsieur Pamplemousse put

the glass down and gazed at it thoughtfully. Perhaps he was wrong to think in terms of wine; perhaps it wasn't so much a matter of *vin rouge*, but rather *hareng rouge*. What the English would call a 'red herring'.

It was largely a matter of what one was conditioned to, of reading what one expected to read. Working as he did for *Le Guide*, his immediate reactions were inclined to be gastronomic. Had he still been with the Sûreté they would have taken him in quite another direction.

Cyanide, *par exemple*?

4

DINNER WITH DUMAS

MONSIEUR PAMPLEMOUSSE GAZED UP AT HIS mount, silhouetted in the cold light from what, given the circumstances, seemed an unnecessarily, not to say an embarrassingly over-bright moon. The horse was not only a good deal bigger than he had expected, it also lacked certain fundamental items of equipment which made his own *deux chevaux* seem, by comparison, positively over-endowed with optional extras; little things like a wheel at all four corners or, more particularly, a handbrake to ensure that it remained stationary when parked. The latter was conspicuous by its absence.

To carry the motoring analogy a stage further, the horse's progenitors had obviously been of like mind to the late Henry Ford, who had offered would-be purchasers of his Model T the choice of any colour under the sun provided they asked for black, for black it certainly was. Black as the ace of spades.

Nor did Monsieur Pamplemousse entirely trust the look in its eyes. Rapport between man and beast seemed fairly low on its agenda for the evening.

'Why is there steam issuing from its nostrils?' he demanded.

'It is mostly the effect of the night air, Monsieur. After the heat of the Opera House . . .' The groom wiped some foam from the horse's lower lip with the back of his sleeve.

'The Opera House?'

'He is appearing all this week in *The Best of Wagner*. Unfortunately, rehearsals this afternoon did not go well. Madame Trenchante, the soprano, is not the lightest of singers, you understand? . . . and the members of the orchestra behaved badly. He is not used to being applauded when he obeys the call of nature. We are hoping for better things at tonight's performance.'

The man suddenly bent down, grasped the offside front leg of the horse with both hands, and gave it a twist. Taken by surprise, the animal promptly lay down on the gravelled driveway.

'See, he is feeling better already!'

Monsieur Pamplemousse had no wish to argue with such an obvious expert in equestrian behaviour, but it struck him as being a very moot point. He was uncomfortably aware of an eye gazing up at him, watching his every move. It was a large eye, unblinking and heavily veined. Set against a colour chart it would have registered yellow rather than white. It struck him as the kind of eye which belonged to an animal merely biding its time until the moment arrived when it could get its own back on those around it.

'That is most kind of you.' Taking a deep breath, he made to clamber on.

'*Monsieur!*' The man grabbed at his arm. 'I would not advise it. Not unless you wish to end up in the river. I was merely demonstrating one of his many tricks, but he is not called *Le Diable Noir* for nothing.'

Monsieur Pamplemousse jumped back. The latest snippet of information did little to assuage his feeling of gloom; a gloom which had set in soon after he left the hotel. The news about the opera explained why there had been so much traffic. In the end he had abandoned all thoughts of using his own car for fear of losing his parking space, choosing instead to walk the half kilometre or so to the Villa André. It also explained why he had been stopped several times on the way for his autograph. He wished now he had taken advantage of the situation. Placido Domingo might have looked even more impressive than Charles de Batz-Castelmore—the name of Dumas' human model for the character of d'Artagnan, and P. Domingo would certainly have been much quicker to write.

The groom relaxed his grip on the horse, withdrew a silver hunting-cased watch from one of has waistcoat pockets, and flicked open the cover with his thumbnail.

'If *Monsieur* will forgive me. It is almost time for the evening performance and we have to be in our places five minutes before the curtain goes up.'

As the horse rose to its feet, Monsieur Pamplemousse looked around for something to stand on—a pair of steps, perhaps? A car roof?—but there was nothing in sight. He glanced towards the house at the end of the short drive. The lights were on and through the open door he could see waiters flitting to and fro. To his relief there was no sign of the photographer the Director had threatened him with. Posterity and Mrs Van Dorman's magazine would have to do without. Taking a deep breath, he braced himself. It was now or never.

'*Monsieur* has ridden before?'

'*Oui*.' Monsieur Pamplemousse dismissed such a foolish question with a wave of his hand. 'Many years ago.' He forbore to mention that the last time—the one and only time—had been on a camel in the Bois de Boulogne. It would have been a sad confession for one born and brought up in the Auvergne.

'Aah!' The tone of voice suggested that his reply was not entirely unexpected. 'Then I would suggest that if *Monsieur* wishes to mount he faces the way he is going so that he can place his other foot in the *trier*.'

Grasping Monsieur Pamplemousse's left foot in much the same manner as he had used earlier in demonstrating his command over the horse, the groom guided it into a stirrup. Then he cupped his hands together to form a step, placed it under the other foot, and gave a quick heave.

It was hard to say which of those present was most surprised by the events which followed, or who reacted the fastest.

Had the promised cameraman been present, and had his finger been on the button, he might have resolved matters by capturing a photo finish with his lens, but he would have needed to be quick for it was all over in a matter of seconds.

Monsieur Pamplemousse, expecting to find himself flying straight over the top of the horse and therefore bracing himself accordingly, met instead with unexpected resistance, spun round, and collapsed in a heap on the driveway.

Pommes Frites, having until that moment remained coldly aloof from the proceedings, sprang into action. Anticipating the outcome by virtue of his vantage point near the ground, he was already at his master's side by the time he landed, his tongue at the ready in case first aid was required.

The horse, taken completely unawares by Monsieur Pamplemousse's sword as it swung round and up, stood for a brief second registering a mixture of shock and disbelief, then gave vent to a cry, more shriek than whinny, before leaping several feet into the air.

Last, but by no means least, although compared to the other three, undoubtedly an also-ran, the groom added his shouts to the *mêlée* as he struggled to regain control of his charge.

'Aristide! Are you all right?'

Groping under a nearby bush for his hat, Monsieur Pamplemousse looked up and found himself gazing into the eyes of Mrs Van Dorman.

'*Oui et non.* I fear I have lost part of my hat.'

'By the sound of it you're lucky if that's all you've lost. I tell you something else. How about we take your entrance as read? The photographer's still tied up inside the house. Besides, we can leave all that until after we've eaten.'

Monsieur Pamplemousse considered the matter for all of a second or two. Mrs Van Dorman wouldn't have to fill in a P.39 at the end of her trip justifying to Madame Grante in Accounts the reasons for claiming a new set of plumes. He doubted very much whether, as an item, they would have been programmed on to *Le Guide*'s computer. There would be innumerable complications. He could picture it all. The section on the form for explanations wouldn't be large enough for a start. Once again he would have to resort to writing 'please see attached sheet'.

He was also distracted from his task by the nearness of Mrs Van Dorman's bosom. She was wearing a high-waisted dark blue dress with a lace-edged off-the-shoulder *décolletage*, the squareness of which emphasised and even enhanced the roundness and fullness of her snowy white *balcons*. *Balcons* which, unlike *Le Diable Noir*, benefitted from being bathed in moonlight. The effect was unexpectedly ravishing, not to say disturbing.

Climbing to his feet with as much grace as possible, Monsieur Pamplemousse adjusted his sword and turned to the groom.

'*Madame* is right. I will see you after the performance. I hope it goes well.'

'*Oui, Monsieur.*' The man sounded as relieved as he did.

Monsieur Pamplemousse glanced at Mrs Van Dorman as they made their way towards the house. 'You are looking very beautiful.'

'Thank you, Aristide. And you are looking very dashing. Doublet and hose suit you. You should always wear them. As for the black beard . . .'

'I think not. It would make life much too complicated in the mornings.'

Monsieur Pamplemousse spoke with feeling. Even with the help of two men from the theatrical costumiers it had taken him most of the afternoon to get ready. As for undressing again, he wouldn't know where to begin. All the same, as he took Mrs Van Dorman's arm he couldn't help feeling a little *je ne sais quoi*—'a certain something'; his step was undoubtedly lighter. His spirits had been raised and he felt on top of the world; it was a night when anything was possible.

Pausing by the steps leading up to the door he became aware, too, of an unseasonable smell of jasmine—jasmine and honeysuckle: strong and heady. It wasn't difficult to locate the source. Mrs Van Dorman read his thoughts.

'I hope you don't find my perfume too overpowering. I picked it up from Jean Laporte when I was in Paris. It belongs to the period—along with the beauty spots.' She pointed to a black patch adorning her right cheek. 'They both served their purpose in covering up bodily imperfections—B. O. and pock-marks. They didn't call Louis XIV a "sweet-smelling monarch" for nothing. He had them build a blue and white pavilion at Versailles and filled it with flowers. They say he used to spend most of his time there—in between bouts of making love.'

'Do you have a perfume for every occasion?'

'I try to. I'm always experimenting. It has to do with the chemistry of the skin. I'll tell you about it some day.

'Anyway, here goes . . .' She led the way into the house and on into the dining-room where two distinct groups were clustered at the far end.

Monsieur Pamplemousse's spirits took a sudden nose-dive again. He'd completely forgotten the thespians the Director had engaged for the occasion. He hoped their expectations of his own acting abilities weren't running too high. If so, they were in for a shock.

Not that it looked as though the expectations of anyone in the room were exactly at fever pitch. As he followed Mrs Van Dorman round the long candle-lit table in the centre of the room, awash with gleaming silver cutlery and sparkling glassware, it struck Monsieur Pamplemousse that the atmosphere was decidedly low key. Apart from their dress, it wasn't hard to distinguish which group was which. The theatricals appeared to be in a state of suspended animation, as though awaiting a cue from some unseen Director before taking the stage. Either that, or they had been given orders not to mingle. The rest of the occupants, perhaps not surprisingly, looked as though they were trying to strike a balance between anticipation of things to come and remembrance of things past.

Someone he recognised as Elliott Garner detached himself from the group of writers and came forward to greet them.

'DiAnn! Or should I say Madame Joyeux? Congratulations. You are looking wonderful.'

'Thank you, Elliott. You haven't met Monsieur Pamplemousse . . . Aristide. And Pommes Frites . . .'

Elliott nodded briefly. 'We saw each other across a crowded kitchen this morning. Although I must admit, I would hardly have recognised you.' His hand felt cold to the touch.

'I am sorry if I have held you up,' said Monsieur Pamplemousse. 'I had a little disagreement with my *cheval*. I feel we may neither of us ever be quite the same again.'

'What is the saying? "Beware of all enterprises that require new clothes." ' Elliott glanced down at Pommes Frites. 'Now I know we are in France.'

Monsieur Pamplemousse looked at him enquiringly.

'In New York dogs are not allowed in restaurants.'

'Now, now, Elliott,' said Mrs Van Dorman. 'Pommes Frites is an honoured guest. Besides, this isn't a restaurant, it's a private gathering.'

'I didn't say he shouldn't be allowed in.' There was

a hint of petulance. 'I was only pointing out one of the differences between our two countries.'

'I think perhaps dogs come under the heading of popular misconceptions,' said Monsieur Pamplemousse. 'Perhaps because of our eating habits, we are not usually thought of as a nation of animal lovers— but *chiens* are almost always welcome. If they weren't people would soon take their custom elsewhere.'

Conscious that Pommes Frites, aware that his name was being taken in vain, had his eye on Elliott Garner as though making notes for future reference, Monsieur Pamplemousse tried to make it crystal clear that if the need arose, he, too, would happily take his custom elsewhere. It was hard to tell if Pommes Frites was grateful or not.

Mrs Van Dorman touched his arm. 'Come and meet the rest of the party, Aristide.'

'Paul Robard . . . Spencer Troon . . . Harman Lock . . . Harvey Wentworth . . .'

Monsieur Pamplemousse took his time. In their formal attire they were hardly recognisable from the pictures he'd seen in the group photograph and he wanted to get them fixed in his mind.

Mrs Van Dorman turned to the second group. 'Alexandre Dumas, I'm sure you know. Madame de Sauvignon, Monsieur Courbet and Monsieur Auguste Maquet.'

Monsieur Pamplemousse eyed them curiously as they bowed and curtsied. It was type-casting with a vengeance. Alexandre Dumas, in his sixties, portly, wearing a waistcoat several sizes too small, beneath which was one of the soft, pleated and embroidered shirts he had made famous; Madame de Sauvignon, slim, poised, undeniably attractive in a long black dress done up at the collar, but with a revealing area of black net across her front; Courbet every inch the 'artist', Maquet, thin-lipped, jealous of Dumas' success, on which he was later to lay claim.

Monsieur Pamplemousse was so taken up with his own responses, making sure he didn't have a second, perhaps even more embarrassing accident with his sword, it was a moment or two before he realised that not one of the second group had spoken a word, and another few seconds before the truth dawned on him. They were all having to mime. For no obvious reason he found the thought immensely cheering. It was probably one of the Director's little economies—or what was perhaps even more likely, having made the Grand gesture, he had encountered opposition from Madame Grante. He could see it all. The endless hair-splitting arguments. The triumphant expression on Madame Grante's face as she had delivered her *coup de grâce*; the fact that actors came a lot cheaper if they didn't have speaking parts.

'You know something.' Harvey Wentworth joined them. 'The last time I was in Paris doing an article for *Gourmet* magazine I took the boat across to that island in the Bois de Boulogne—the one with the restaurant. There's a notice by the ferry saying dogs are forbidden unless they are going there to eat! Can you imagine that happening back in the States?'

'A few yeas ago,' said Monsieur Pamplemousse, 'someone opened a restaurant in Nice for dogs only.'

'No kidding? What happened if one of them brought an owner in?'

'He got chained to the table like the rest of them,' said Spencer Troon.

Everyone laughed.

'Let's drink to that.' Harvey took a ladle from a silver bowl on the sideboard and filled a glass with a sepia-coloured liquid. 'Punch *à l' Alexandre Dumas*. One of his own inventions. Perfected over years of party giving.'

Monsieur Pamplemousse took the glass and held it to his nose. He hazarded a quick guess. 'Lemon tea? Lemon tea with something much more potent added.'

'Right in one. If you want a repeat order when you get back home—put some sugar into a large bowl and mix in some rum. Light the blue touch paper and stir until it reduces to a third. Add hot Souchong tea and some lemon juice, then top up with mystery ingredient "X"—white Batavian arrack.'

'I wouldn't bother writing it down,' said Paul Robard, 'the recipe'll be in Harvey's next book.'

'So?' Harvey looked unabashed. 'Something new comes your way—you use it. That's what it's all about, right? Old "motormouth" Norm himself would have been on to it like a shot. He's probably making notes even now.'

'In all that heat?' Paul Robard gave a snort.

Harman Lock drained his glass. 'Let us not speak ill of the dear departed.'

The ice broken, everyone suddenly began talking at once, and finding some of the accents difficult to follow Monsieur Pamplemousse took the opportunity to cast his eye over the wine on a sideboard to his right. With the exception of some white burgundy and a bottle or two of Loire poking out from a pair of large ice-buckets, it was all from Bordeaux. He caught sight of a Mouton-Rothschild and a Château Léoville. In the centre of the sideboard, in a position of honour, stood a decanting machine with a bottle already in place. The original label had long since disappeared, but he couldn't resist looking at a hand-written tag dangling from the neck.

Elliott came up behind him. 'You approve?'

'Lafite 1884? How could I not?'

'I acquired it for the occasion at a wine auction in California. It is our one big extravagance for the evening. I tell myself Dumas would have approved. He was an extremely generous host.'

He was also, thought Monsieur Pamplemousse, a teetotaller. Clearly, Elliott wasn't living up to his reputation of being meticulous on research. He let it pass, deciding instead to watch out for other mistakes. Elliott invited a challenge.

'Where did you learn about this particular event?'

Elliott shrugged. 'I don't even remember. Someone must have told me. As I'm sure you know only too well, research often throws up all kinds of strange facts.'

'I congratulate you on the Lafite. It is a great coup.'

'I read somewhere that it was the favourite drink of Queen Victoria. The cellar book at Windsor Castle lists the 1862 vintage as being the house wine.'

'She has gone up in my estimation,' said Monsieur Pamplemousse. 'I had always pictured her as being a little *formidable*.'

'It only goes to show. Things are seldom what they seem.' Elliott ran his eyes over the other bottles, making a last-minute check that all was well.

'Ideally, it would have been nice if all the wines could have been of the period, but there is a limit. However, I suspect namewise they would have been much as you see here. It was the beginning of a golden age for Bordeaux. The 1855 classification had just taken place and the vines had yet to be stricken by phyloxera. Mouton-Rothschild had begun its long fight to be recognised as a first growth—it was fetching the same prices, and Léoville already belonged to an Irish family named Barton.'

'You must have done a lot of research.'

'It's fun. And you learn a lot on the way.'

'It has been said that *Les Trois Mousquetaires* could not have been written without all the research carried out by Auguste Maquet.'

Elliott Garner looked at him with interest. 'You're a scholar of Dumas?'

Monsieur Pamplemousse shook his head. 'Only from around forty-eight hours ago. As a child I was brought up on *The Count of Monte Cristo*, but I have a lot of catching up to do.'

The reply was casual enough, but somehow he sensed a momentary feeling of relief in the other. It would have been hard to put into words, and in any case further conversation was cut short by the sound of a dinner gong from the other end of the room.

He looked at his watch. It was exactly eight o'clock.

As they made their way towards the table Elliott motioned the actor playing Dumas to sit at the head. 'I feel that is where you should be. I have put your mistress, Madame de Sauvignon, on your right. Paul, you are next to her, then Harman and Auguste Maquet.'

'I guess we're going to have to talk to each other, Paul,' said Harman.

'You win some, you lose some.' Paul Robard looked as though he would be perfectly happy if he spent the evening miming to Madame de Sauvignon. Harman was in for a thin time.

'I shall be at the other end of the table,' continued Elliott. 'On my right, Monsieur Courbet. Then Harvey, Madame Joyeux, Monsieur d'Artagnan, and Spencer.'

Almost imperceptibly a bevy of waiters moved into position. Chairs were pulled back, then rearranged as the guests seated themselves.

As the waiters disappeared to begin preparations for serving the first course, the *sommelier* and his assistant began pouring the wine. Monsieur Pamplemousse had to admire Elliott's attention to detail. All the same, he couldn't resist a dig as the waiters reappeared.

'I see the service is *à la Russe*. Does that mean you won your battle this morning?'

Elliott looked at him in surprise. 'Of course.'

'Beware of Elliott,' said Harman. 'Elliott treats any form of disagreement as a confrontation and he has to come out top. Right, Elliott?'

Elliott didn't even bother to reply.

'*Potage à la Crevette, Monsieur.*' One of the waiters moved in alongside Monsieur Pamplemousse and served him from a tureen.

'Another of Dumas' own inventions,' said Elliott, for the benefit of the assembly. 'He adored shellfish—shrimps especially.

'He made it with tomatoes, onions, white wine and the *bouillon* from a *pot au feu*. The tomatoes and onions are cooked in one pan, the shrimps with white wine in another. He always added a pinch of sugar to bring out the flavour of the tomato. I'm sure when you taste it you will agree the amalgamation is superb.'

While Elliott was talking, Monsieur Pamplemousse sipped the wine. It was a Pouilly Fumé: deliciously flinty. Its bouquet mingled perfectly with that of the soup.

He settled back and tried to make himself comfortable. Dressed in all his finery, it wasn't easy. Already there was a large smear of butter on his right sleeve. He looked around for some bread. D'Artagnan would probably have speared some from across the table with his sword. Monsieur Pamplemousse resisted the temptation.

The soup brought back memories of his childhood: the *bouillon* from Sunday's *pot au feu* which appeared as a base for other dishes all through the week. If the rest of the meal lived up to its early promise, then as a *restaurateur* Elliott would undoubtedly have been in line for a Stock Pot or two in *Le Guide*.

'Boy, this is something.' Harvey Wentworth smacked his lips.

'Dumas was lucky to have lived by the sea during an age of abundance,' said Monsieur Pamplemousse. 'Food was there for the taking and it was going to last for ever.'

'The field which ploughs itself,' said Elliott. 'And it's cheap. Compare an acre of the Atlantic with an acre anywhere in the States. But for years people ignored the fact that it still has to be sown.'

'It's the same all over the world,' agreed Harman. 'When I was a kid in California you couldn't walk on the beach without treading on clams. Now they fine you if you're caught picking them up under a certain size.'

'You know something?' said Harvey. 'Take crabs, right? You get on an airline and what do they serve you? Crab meat, right? Or lobster. You know where most of it comes from? The Orient. They call it "blended sea-food product" which is supposed to make it OK, right? But what you're really eating is cod, plus starch, chemical seasoning and boiled down crab shells to give it the flavour. It's got to be big business, but the sad thing is people will grow up thinking it's the real thing.'

The *Lamproie à la Bordelaise* came and went while everyone started talking at once about the difficulties of living in such a profligate, uncaring world. Monsieur Pamplemousse decided it was probably a good thing. Prepared in the traditional way, the story of the lamprey's journey from the Gironde to the plate was not for the gastronomically faint-hearted, even if in many people's eyes the end justified the means.

He concentrated instead on the second wine; a Grand Cru Chablis from the Domaine de la Maladière. Palish yellow in colour, with just a hint of green, it was steely dry, and richly perfumed without being cloying. From choice, he would have preferred a red; it would have gone better with the dark sauce made from the lamprey's own blood, but he wasn't grumbling.

The asparagus tips which followed were served with scrambled eggs to which a chicken *bouillon* had been added. It was a very smooth combination. Monsieur Pamplemousse reached instinctively for the notepad he normally kept concealed in his right trouser leg. As he did so he encountered a wet nose.

The sigh of contentment which emerged from beneath the table as he took the hint and delivered a sizable portion on a piece of bread didn't pass unnoticed. It was rewarded with a second helping.

Elliott called across. 'Don't tell me Monsieur d'Artagnan is flagging already. You disappoint me.'

'On the contrary. Pommes Frites is very fond of *asperge*. I was interested in his views.'

'You want my views?' Harman Lock broke off from

a conversation he'd been having with Paul Robard. 'I reckon it's a good thing Norm wasn't here tonight. If drinking spa water did for him he would have died of a heart attack twice over by now.'

Monsieur Pamplemousse shrugged. 'Perhaps. They thought the Emperor Claudius died of indigestion through eating too many mushrooms until they found that whoever tickled his throat to make him vomit had used a poisoned feather.'

Harvey Wentworth leaned forward and looked along the table. 'What are you trying to say?' he demanded. 'That Norm didn't have heart failure?'

'No. Only that until the result of the post mortem no one knows why it stopped beating. It could have been for a variety of reasons.'

'It's the one certain thing that happens when we die,' agreed Paul.

'He didn't need the insurance money, that's for sure,' broke in Spencer Troon. 'I heard he got an advance of over a quarter of a million bucks for his next three books. A quarter of a million bucks without a word being written, would you believe?'

'I know one person who'll be in deep mourning at the funeral,' said Harman. 'His agent. I doubt if he's gotten a single word on paper.'

'He was probably waiting to see what we did next before he got started,' said Paul.

'I don't know so much,' said Harvey. 'At least he came up with something original before he died. Can you imagine having "Bring me a bottle of Bâtard Montrachet and some fish" written on your tombstone?'

Monsieur Pamplemousse caught Mrs Van Dorman's eye. She gave a slight shrug as much as to say 'What did I tell you?'

'Hey, fellers . . .' It was Harman Lock. 'Can't we talk about something else tonight?'

Elliott rapped his knife against a glass, calling the table to order.

'Harman's right. It's time for the *ortolans*. In a moment I will ask you to cover your heads in the traditional manner. Special napkins will be provided. But before that . . .' he glanced along the table towards Monsieur Pamplemousse, 'perhaps our honoured guest would like to tell you something about them. In his role of d'Artagnan they can be said to inhabit his part of the country, and I understand that in real life he is something of an expert.'

Monsieur Pamplemousse wasn't sure whether it was an attempt to put him down, or whether he was being paid a compliment. He decided to give Elliott the benefit of the doubt.

'I have to admit I have never eaten them—the nearest I have experienced is larks, but they are really at their best in winter. In the Auvergne, when I was a boy, I used to see *ortolans* fly over twice a year—in May and October. Once *en route* to Burgundy where they built their nests in the vineyards, and again on their way back south after the breeding season.'

He glanced towards Elliott. 'I must congratulate you on your detective work. In Alexandre Dumas' time they were a symbol of richness. Nowadays, like the fish we were talking about earlier, they have become something of a rarity. Tracking them down cannot have been easy.'

In view of the conversation round the table he was sorely tempted to point to a moral about shared guilt, but he decided that would be out of place.

As his dish was placed before him he was pleased to see that the birds had been cooked in the simplest way possible; wrapped in vine leaves and roasted in a pan rather than on a spit. There were three to a plate, resting on slices of toast. Each bird had a quarter of lemon beside it.

The *sommelier* offered up two bottles of wine. Monsieur Pamplemousse chose the Mouton in preference to the Léoville, then leaned back while a waiter tied a fresh napkin over his head. It was like the preparation for a sacred rite, which indeed it was in some people's eyes.

He felt a pressure against his left leg. Patently it didn't emanate from Pommes Frites. Pommes Frites wasn't given to sending messages in that way; the placing of a paw on the foot or knee perhaps, but not lingeringly on the calf. He glanced along at Mrs Van Dorman, but she had already disappeared beneath her napkin. It was hard to say whether she had been trying to attract his attention about something or was looking for support. Perhaps she didn't like the sight of small birds peering up at her. A sudden movement by Madame de Sauvignon on the other side of the table suggested that others were taking advantage of the situation.

The toast had been prepared by first cooking it in goose fat and afterwards spreading it with Roquefort cheese. It would test Alexandre Dumas' theory about raisins to the limit.

As he placed both hands beneath the canopy his napkin had formed over the *ortolans* and began dissecting the birds, Monsieur Pamplemousse found himself wondering about the evening. Mrs Van Dorman was wrong about one thing. It wasn't so much that her party bickered amongst themselves, rather that they all shared a common dislike of the late, but obviously not greatly lamented, Norm Ellis.

His first reaction on hearing of Ellis's death had been that he must have committed suicide. But if that were the case, it was a slightly bizarre way of going about it. On the surface he had everything to live for, but success didn't necessarily bring happiness, and as Elliott had so rightly said, things weren't always what they seemed. All the same, in his experience potential suicides very rarely used cyanide; in fact in all his time in the force, he couldn't remember having come across such a case.

Peeling off a piece of meat, he reached under the table, but Pommes Frites was no longer there.

Pommes Frites, in fact, had gone on a voyage of exploration. There were certain matters to attend to; things he wanted to get straight in his mind before he was very much older. Pommes Frites had an orderly, almost computer-like mind. It relied on the breaking down of problems into a series of short questions to which the answer was either yes or no. 'Perhaps' and 'maybe' were not words which formed part of his vocabulary, and there were currently too many of both for his liking.

Unaware of the reason for Pommes Frites' absence, Monsieur Pamplemousse consumed the offering himself, then took the opportunity to feel for his glass. Anyway, why choose Vichy of all places? Unless, of course, Ellis was going to extreme lengths to make it appear as though he had died from natural causes. Insurance perhaps? It hardly seemed likely. People committing suicide were seldom that thoughtful of the effect it would have on others, and he hardly seemed in great need.

The wine was rich and opulent, with an aroma of ripe plums and spicy oak. It was Mouton at its best.

And if Ellis hadn't committed suicide, what then?

93

That thought and the ones which followed on took on a slightly eerie aspect in the circumstances. Sitting with his head in a shroud made him feel vulnerable, as he always did in a shower during the moment when his eyes were closed to protect them from the soap. Perhaps Mrs Van Dorman had been feeling it too and that was why she had reached out. He decided a call to the Poison Control Centre in Paris in the morning would not come amiss; although quite what he would ask them was another matter.

Quickly polishing off the remains of the dish, Monsieur Pamplemousse uncovered his face and reached for a finger bowl. He was the first to finish. The neat pile of tiny bones on his plate looked as though they had been picked clean by a hungry buzzard and then left to whiten in the desert sun.

Out of the corner of his eye he caught an approving look from the waiter as he removed the napkin from around his neck.

One by one the others emerged from beneath their hoods. Mrs Van Dorman was next. The heat had brought a flush to her cheeks. The beauty patch on her cheek seemed to have slipped slightly. It was probably one of the hazards of the period. He reached up and felt his beard to make sure it was still in place.

Feeling that some kind of comment was due, he called across to Elliott. 'My compliments to the chef. Brillat-Savarin was right: "One becomes a cook, but one is born a roasting cook." '

Mrs Van Dorman looked at her own plate. 'I have a feeling I'm not going to make the finishing line,' she whispered.

Monsieur Pamplemousse glanced round the table. 'I think you are not the only one.'

'You do this kind of thing *every* day? For a living? How do you manage it?'

Monsieur Pamplemousse shrugged. 'All occupations have their hazards. I rarely accept second helpings. Sometimes I follow the example set by one of our rivals—Monsieur Christian Millau. He insists on being given half portions wherever he goes. When it is possible, I drink a glass of fresh carrot juice half an hour before a meal. It is very effective provided it is fresh—not bottled. And since I started reading Alexandre Dumas I have taken to carrying raisins for afterwards.'

'And they work?'

'I will tell you tomorrow. In between I rely on Pommes Frites. He never lets me down.' He was about to amend that to 'rarely', then thought better of it.

Mrs Van Dorman looked past him. 'I know one person who's enjoying himself. He hasn't been so quiet all evening.'

Monsieur Pamplemousse glanced to his right where a waiter was hovering behind the one remaining guest still wearing a shroud. Catching the man's eye, he gave a brief nod. Others bearing trays laden with sorbets were already waiting outside the door, and he could sense Elliott's impatience at the hold-up. No doubt he was anxious to reach the high spot of the evening—the *Rôtie à l'Impératrice*.

Neatly and deftly the waiter undid the knot holding the napkin in place and with a barberlike flourish shook it free. As he did so, almost as though he had withdrawn a cork from a bottle, there came an unearthly groan which sent a shiver round the room. For a moment there was total silence as the rest of those around the table stared aghast, then someone—it must have been Madame de Sauvignon—let out a scream.

Jumping to his feet, Monsieur Pamplemousse reached out, but he was a fraction of a second too late. With a crash which sent china and glass flying, Spencer Troon hit the table and lay motionless where he had landed. The dribble of blood which oozed from his lips mingled with the half-eaten remains of the *Ortolans à la Landaise*, giving the effect not so much of a classic dish of days gone by, but *nouvelle cuisine* at its most macabre.

With a sense of timing perfected over the years, Pommes Frites chose that particular moment to return from his wanderings. Taking in the situation at a glance he lifted his head and added his mite to Madame de Sauvignon's scream of horror. As a howl, it was not so much one of alarm or grief, but rather of indignation. The indignation of one who felt that if only he had been consulted earlier all this might not have happened.

5

THE LONE STRANGER

'OF ALL THE GODDAMN CRAZY THINGS!' ELLIOTT looked as though he was about to burst a blood vessel. Monsieur Pamplemousse had seldom seen anyone so furious. He was positively white with rage.

'And what's with all the tomato ketchup?'

Spencer Troon, dabbing at his mouth with a napkin, looked bloody but unbowed.

'How the hell should I know? I haven't worked that bit out yet. Anyway, if you want to know, it isn't tomato ketchup. I got it from a joke shop in town.'

'I haven't worked that bit out yet,' mimicked Elliott. 'Typical! It's like everything else you do.'

'These things take time,' said Spencer. 'You should know that. Maybe I had a poisoned bone. Like that story Aristide here told about the feather.' He turned to Monsieur Pamplemousse for help. 'What was the guy's name? That Emperor . . . the one who ate too many mushrooms?'

'Claudius?' Monsieur Pamplemousse was still recovering from his surprise—he wouldn't have admitted to the word shock—at finding Spencer return from the dead as it were. The whole episode had a strange surrealistic feel to it. One moment he'd been lying sprawled across the table looking as though he had breathed his last, the next moment he'd jumped to his feet uttering a triumphant cry as though nothing had happened. The others seemed to share Elliott's irritation, and he had to agree with them. In the circumstances it seemed a particularly tasteless joke to play.

'That's the one,' said Spencer. 'Claudius. He had a poisoned feather with his number on, right? So—in my case it was a bone. Like with Norm. Norm's number was called. That's why he's up there working away at the Great Word-Processor in the sky, right?'

'Jesus!' said Harman. 'Why can't you just say he's dead. How many different ways are there of not saying it?'

'You name it,' broke in Paul Robard, 'they come up with it. "Non-viable condition"; "negative patient care outcome"; "paying a call on the perpetual rest consultant"; "patient failed to fulfil his wellness potential". They've got a million.'

'You're right there,' conceded Harman. 'Anything to pass the buck. You know, I even read the other day of a guy who took an overdose and put himself into a "non-decision-making mode". Can you beat that? The poor sap tries to end it all and what do they call it? A "non-decision-making mode". Decisions don't come any bigger than wanting to do away with yourself.'

'What happened to him?' asked Harvey Wentworth.

'They botched the treatment. Some intern took a decision for him and it just so happened it was the wrong one. He suffered a "negative mortality experience". In other words, same as Norm. He died.'

'What the hell?' said Spencer. 'I had you all fooled there for a moment and somebody had to be runner-up. I know one thing, though. If Norm *is* working away at his word-processor, the rest of us are going to suffer "inventory shrinkage" when it comes to stock-appraisal time.'

Elliott gave a deep, deep sigh as he rose to his feet. 'I suggest we change the subject. I refuse to allow the evening to be spoilt because of a petty, childish prank.'

He crossed to the sideboard where the *sommelier* had placed a lighted candle behind the neck of the bottle held in the decanting machine. The cork had been drawn some time previously. A row of seven glasses arranged alongside the machine provided an answer to another of Monsieur Pamplemousse's earlier unspoken questions. The thespians were having to do without. He could hardly blame Elliott. Considering what the wine must have cost it would be carrying generosity a bit far to share it amongst the whole table, although from the look on one or two of the actors' faces it was not a view shared by all. Alexandre Dumas in particular had so far forgotten his role that he was looking most aggrieved. Method acting was obviously not his particular forte.

'Anyway,' Elliott bent down and cranked the handle very gently until almost imperceptibly the bottle, already some ten degrees or so off the vertical, began to tilt still further, 'we're all wasting our breath. The contest is null and void.'

'What do you mean—null and void?' exclaimed Spencer. 'I chipped in the same as everyone else.'

'Ssh!' Aware that the *sommelier* was casting a critical eye over his right shoulder, watching his every move, Elliott was not disposed to argue.

'Do what the man says,' broke in Harman. 'Can't you see he's busy.'

While all eyes turned to watch Elliott at work, the sorbet arrived, replacing the absinthe of Dumas' day.

'It is a lemon *granité*, *Monsieur*,' whispered the waiter with evident approval. 'It is made with the addition of a little *anisette*.'

'Jesus!' exclaimed Paul Robard as he took a mouthful. 'What are they trying to do—poison us?'

Monsieur Pamplemousse tasted a little. Judged simply as a palate cleanser it was undervaluing itself. A confirmed alcoholic would have been kept happy for days; a furniture restorer would have looked no further for some polish remover. No wonder the waiter's hand had been a little shaky.

He pondered over the conversation that had just taken place, wishing once again that his command of the language was better. It was hard to tell what the others were thinking; the dialogue might well have been lifted out of any of their books—delivered in a brittle, poker-faced fashion. But beneath it all he sensed undeniable nuances and undercurrents, the true meaning of which escaped him for the moment. He resolved to question Mrs Van Dorman later. In the meantime he broke off a piece of bread and chewed it for a moment or two in order to take away the taste of the *granité*.

'I suggest we all do the same,' said Elliott approvingly, as he returned to the table and stood hovering like a mother hen over her chicks while the waiter distributed the glasses.

Monsieur Pamplemousse studied his own offering for a moment or two, almost afraid to touch it in case the contents of the glass disappeared or he shook up some vital element which would cause the wine to break up. Elliott had done a good job. Not only had he managed to extract seven moderate servings from the bottle, but the liquid was crystal clear with no tell-tale traces of murkiness which would have occurred had any of the sediment been disturbed during the pouring.

He picked up his glass and held it at arm's length. The wine was a deep amber colour. It showed well against the soft candle-light. The glass was a Riedel Bordeaux—shaped so as to enhance the wine rather than show up its defects, throwing the contents towards the back of the mouth and away from the tip of the tongue and the 'sweet' taste buds.

The Director would have envied him, in fact most of those who had wangled their way out of the assignment would have envied him at that moment. It served them right.

He was soon so lost in thought he was hardly aware of the *Rôtie à l'Impératrice* arriving.

It must have tested the chef to the full; not only in the preparation and the cooking, but in the serving of it as well. It must have been no easy matter to ensure that everyone received their fair share of all the component parts; the *porc*, the turkey, the pheasant, the partridge, the quail and the lark. The juice came separately in silver serving bowls, along with a simple salad of fresh dandelion leaves; it was exactly right; anything more would have been unnecessary—a case of over-gilding the lily, and the slightly bitter taste would counterbalance the richness of the dish.

'The next question', said Elliott, 'is whether we drink the wine by itself or savour it along with what is, after all, the main event of the evening. Aristide, what do you think?'

Once again Monsieur Pamplemousse had the feeling he was being tested. 'In my view,' he said, 'a wine such as this deserves our full attention. Look at that colour.' He held the glass to his nose. It was rich and fragrant; spicy. 'And smell the bouquet.'

He paused for a moment. 'It is *formidable* . . . *merveilleux*. I think we should, perhaps, do both. Drink a little of the wine by itself first, then test it against the *rôtie*. In that way we can have the best of both worlds and there will be no argument afterwards.'

The truth of the matter was he would have been more than happy just to savour the wine. It would be a memorable way of rounding off the evening. He had a feeling the *Rôtie à l'Impératrice* might come under the heading of 'experiences I have known' or possibly even 'experiences I wish I hadn't known'. It represented the worst excesses of the period. Contemplating his plate, he was reminded of the time when he had taken Doucette to see a film called *La Grande Bouffe*. They hadn't wanted to eat for days afterwards. Now the thought had entered his mind he couldn't rid himself of it, and he was relieved when he felt a stirring at his feet. Even if he had been an avid cinema goer, Pommes Frites would have suffered no such inhibitions.

'Spoken like a true diplomat,' said Elliott. 'D'Artagnan himself couldn't have put it better. How about the bouquet? Has anyone got any ideas?'

'I guess I can pick up some kind of spices,' said Harman. 'Don't ask me what.'

'I get a bit of Eucalyptus,' said Harvey.

'A touch of resin, maybe?' Paul Robard hazarded a guess.

'I'd go for raspberries,' said Spencer. 'Raspberries and currants—fruit anyway.'

'DiAnn?'

'I think I would agree about the fruit,' said Mrs Van Dorman. 'But there are so many things. Does anyone else get almond? It comes over quite strongly in my glass.'

There was a murmur of dissent from around the table. Suddenly alert, Monsieur Pamplemousse leaned forward.

Mrs Van Dorman raised the glass to her lips. 'Well someone has to start, I guess.'

'Attention!' Leaping to his feet, Monsieur Pamplemousse made a grab for Mrs Van Dorman's hand. Somehow or other, as she jerked back her head the glass eluded him and flew out of her hand. As it landed with a crash on Elliott's plate, a rivulet of dark red liquid slowly spread out across the table.

For a second or two everyone sat in stunned silence. Pommes Frites was the first to move. He put his front paws on the table, gave the remains of the wine a desultory sniff, then settled himself down alongside his master to await further developments. They weren't long in coming.

Elliott rose to his feet. 'I don't know what occasioned that behaviour, nor do I wish to ruin what until now has been a thoroughly delightful evening by enquiring into the matter further. I assume you had good reasons for behaving as you did . . .'

Monsieur Pamplemousse also rose. 'I can assure

103

you, Monsieur Garner, I had very good reasons, although I would rather not elaborate on them at this moment in time. Please accept my sincere apologies.'

Elliott gave a brief nod. 'I think we are all a little on edge this evening.'

'I hope . . .' Monsieur Pamplemousse picked up his own glass and handed it to Mrs Van Dorman, 'I hope Madame Joyeux will accept this in recompense.' It was the least he could do.

'I won't say no to sharing.'

Elliott left the table. 'If you will excuse me . . . I must go and wipe myself down. Please carry on.'

Suddenly you could feel the relief in the air as Elliott left the room.

'If that was me,' said Harman Lock, 'I'd be wanting to squeegee my pants into the nearest glass.'

'There'll be a third thing,' said Paul darkly, as he speared a mouthful of meat with his fork. 'Any guesses as to what it'll be?'

There were no takers.

It was, to all intents and purposes, the end of the evening. For all its uniqueness, the *Rôtie à l'Impératrice* came as something of an anti-climax. There were no takers for a second helping.

By the time Elliott returned, most of the guests were either ready for the next course, or only too willing to do without it. The peaches in wine had few takers. Sadly, Monsieur Pamplemousse watched his pears with bacon begin its journey back to the kitchen, untouched even by Pommes Frites. The cheese board followed swiftly in its wake. Coffee was a muted affair. The farewell speech by Elliott and the vote of thanks by Mrs Van Dorman, were both mercifully brief.

'What did you make of all that?' asked Monsieur

Pamplemousse as they took their leave of the others and headed towards the door.

'I thought Elliott took it remarkably well. I felt so sorry for him. Do you know how much that bottle cost? They say he nursed it all across the Atlantic. Sat with it between his knees and wouldn't let it out of his sight. It's almost as bad as that time at the Four Seasons in New York when a waiter hit a bottle of 1787 Château Margaux with his tray. Remember? Over four hundred thousand dollars of wine disappeared into the carpet.'

'Indeed I do.' It wasn't what he'd meant, but clearly Mrs Van Dorman was blissfully unaware of the fact that for a moment he had feared for her life.

'What came over you? I couldn't believe my eyes.'

Monsieur Pamplemousse wondered if he should tell the truth—it was hard to know how she would take it—but as they were about to leave the house she abruptly changed the subject.

'Oh, God! I'd completely forgotten. We have a reception committee.'

'I have been wondering,' said the photographer, 'if perhaps we should try something in *contre-jour*. *Madame* could stand exactly where she is . . . perhaps a little further out . . . so that she is framed in the doorway with the light behind . . . a handkerchief in her hand to stem the tears as she waves goodbye. *Monsieur* can be in the foreground, mounting his charger.'

Monsieur Pamplemousse considered the idea for a moment. He could think of no very good reason why d'Artagnan would have wished to leave his mistress at that moment—unless, of course, another adventure called. On the other hand, flushed with good food, awash with even better wine—the memory of his share of the Lafite '84 still lingering in his mouth—he felt in an obliging mood.

'Whatever you suggest. *Pas de problème!*'

Mrs Van Dorman opened a small purse she had been carrying all the evening and searched for something suitable to wave. 'Do be careful, Aristide. Remember what happened last time.'

'This time,' said the groom, 'I have brought a *montoir*—a mounting block.'

'You see,' said Monsieur Pamplemousse, as he accepted the other's outstretched hand. 'It is as I said . . . *pas de problème.*'

'I have also taken the precaution of fitting *Le Diable Noir* with blinkers so that he cannot see you,' said the man. He sounded anxious to get to bed.

Pommes Frites did a double-take as he joined Mrs Van Dorman in the doorway and contemplated the scene before him.

'Excellent!' exclaimed the photographer. 'The finishing touch! *Ne quittez pas, s'il vous plaît!*'

In assuming that Pommes Frites had taken up the pose of a hunter ready to spring into action at a moment's notice simply because he wished to be in the picture, the photographer was doing him a grave injustice. Pommes Frites was not so much riveted to the spot for artistic reasons as glued to it because he could hardly believe what was going on. Although in the normal course of events Monsieur Pamplemousse could do no wrong in Pommes Frites' eyes, if questioned on the subject he would have been forced to admit that there were moments when in his humble opinion his master came very close to pushing his luck a bit too far. Patently this was one of those occasions.

But even Pommes Frites was hardly prepared for the events of the next few seconds.

Emboldened on the one hand by the wine, and if he'd been totally honest, a sudden desire to impress Mrs Van Dorman, Monsieur Pamplemousse flung caution to the wind. As a schoolboy he had learned the lesson that bravery is often a mixture of foolhardiness coupled with the fear of being laughed at. Given something nobody really wants to do, there are positive advantages in being first to have a go; at least you get it over with. In that way he had gained something of a reputation for bravery; leading the rest of the class into the water when it was time for a swimming lesson on a cold winter's day, or being first up a tree when a kite became entangled in its uppermost branches.

It was in much the same spirit that he snatched the purse from Mrs Van Dorman and in one swift movement leapt into the air, landing more by luck than judgement fairly and squarely in the middle of the saddle.

For the second time that evening the photographer missed his big moment. There was no possibility of another chance. As Monsieur Pamplemousse landed on its back, *Le Diable Noir* gave a loud whinny and reared into the air like a bucking bronco determined to free itself of its rider. The fact that horse and rider remained as one was simply because Monsieur Pamplemousse had got his own impedimenta entangled with that of his steed. Clutching Mrs Van Dorman's purse in one hand, holding on like grim death to the *pommeau* with his other, stirrups flying in the wind, he disappeared down the drive and out through the open gate as though shot from a canon.

A moment later Pommes Frites woke from his trance and set off in hot pursuit.

Whichever of Monsieur Pamplemousse's guardian angels was unlucky enough to be taking the late shift that night must have been torn between watching over his charge and keeping an up-to-the-minute record of the events which followed. Doubtless in the circumstances he was forgiven for lapsing into some kind of heavenly shorthand.

X'd boulevard Pres. Kennedy. Entered Parc du Soleil by r. On to D426 then N. on to D270 and D175.

Had he dared, Monsieur Pamplemousse would gladly have swopped Mrs Van Dorman's purse for *Le Diable Noir*'s blinkers.

As they headed towards open country the telephone in the local *gendarmerie* began to ring. It was the first of many calls from late-night motorists and startled householders wakened by the clatter of hooves. But by the time it was answered Monsieur Pamplemousse was already lying in a ditch. The Monts de la Madeleine, which only that morning had seemed so far away, now loomed uncomfortably close.

Thankful to be alive and in one piece, he lay for some while where he had landed. Mercifully the ditch was devoid of water. It was even, by comparison with the saddle, remarkably soft and comfortable and he had no great desire to move.

Gradually growing accustomed to his surroundings and having assured himself that there were no broken bones, Monsieur Pamplemousse relaxed. As he did so he became aware of the sound of an approaching car. Struggling into a sitting position, he gave a desultory wave. Almost immediately he wished he hadn't.

Temporarily blinded by the headlights, which remained pointing straight at him as the car skidded to a halt, Monsieur Pamplemousse raised an arm to shield his eyes from the glare.

It was too late to hide. Hands reached out and helped him clamber to his feet. There was a pause while he recovered his balance and then the first of the two *gendarmes* spoke.

'*Monsieur*, may I see your papers?'

'I have no papers,' said Monsieur Pamplemousse. 'At least, not on me. They are in my hotel room.'

The men exchanged glances. 'Your name, *Monsieur*?' enquired the second gendarme.

Monsieur Pamplemousse essayed an attempt at the jocular. 'I am Charles de Batz-Castelmore, but you may call me d'Artagnan.'

'*Oui, Monsieur*,' said the first, 'and I am Robespierre.'

Monsieur Pamplemousse recognised the type. Sound in many ways. Painstaking. Given the right instructions, he would be indefatigable in following up an inquiry. But no sense of humour whatsoever.

'All right,' he said wearily. 'My name is Pamplemousse. Late of the Sûreté.'

The two men looked at each other again. '*Oui, Monsieur*,' said the second one. 'Now, will you please turn around.'

Monsieur Pamplemousse knew better than to argue. He would have done the same thing in their place; a quick frisk to check for concealed weapons; no guns concealed in the ruff, no hidden knives. Better safe than sorry. There was room for a whole armoury inside his sleeves. He waited patiently while the officer subjected him to a brief body search. First the top half, then the lower. Suddenly he felt his arms being grasped from behind. There was a tightening round his wrists followed by a series of rapid clicks.

109

'*Sacré bleu!*' He struggled to free himself, but it was too late.

'What is the meaning of this?'

'The meaning, *Monsieur*,' said the first gendarme, 'is quite simple. You are under arrest.'

'Arrest? On what charge?'

'You really wish to know?' The man's voice sounded pained. He turned to his colleague for support. 'First of all he terrorises half the neighbourhood by rampaging through the streets at one o'clock in the morning on a horse. Then he is found lying in a ditch wearing fancy dress and smelling of drink. Next he gives a series of false names . . . And he wants to know why we are arresting him!'

The second gendarme gave a hollow laugh.

'All right,' said Monsieur Pamplemousse. He could see there was little point in arguing. 'I can explain it all when we get to the station. But in the meantime— what about my horse?'

'Your horse, *Monsieur*? What horse?'

Monsieur Pamplemousse nodded towards a small clump of trees on the far side of the road. 'He is somewhere over there. You can hardly leave him to roam around loose all night. Who knows what damage he may cause?

'*Ici! Ici!*' Warming to his theme, he emitted a series of whistles which, if they did nothing else, produced a satisfactory and clearly recognisable response from further down the road. A single bark indicated that Pommes Frites wasn't far away.

'*Attendez un moment, Monsieur.*'

The possibility that he might do anything other than wait clearly didn't enter the minds of the *gendarmes* as they crossed the road. One of them produced a torch and began waving it around in a desultory fashion.

Monsieur Pamplemousse held back until they reached the trees, then he turned and took a flying leap across the ditch. As he landed on the far side he slipped on the turf. For a brief moment he thought he was going to fall. Then, regaining his balance with an almost superhuman effort, he was away. Oblivious to the shouts calling him to stop or else, he set off across the open country as fast as he could.

From somewhere behind him he heard the sound of barking; barking followed by snarls. There were several shrill blasts on a whistle, then silence. By the sound of things Pommes Frites was doing his bit.

Monsieur Pamplemousse wasn't sure how long he carried on running; it was probably only a matter of minutes, but it seemed like hours. Heart pounding, his breath becoming shorter with every passing moment, he kept going; across fields, in and out of ditches, over rocks, until gradually the running dwindled into a jog, and the jog into a walk. Finally, stumbling over a boulder, he sat down in order to regain his breath.

He still wasn't sure quite why he had done it. Instinct; a spur of the moment decision. But he'd burned his boats and no mistake.

The irony of the situation suddenly struck home. He, Aristide Pamplemousse, late of the Sûreté, on the run like a common criminal. It was too late to do anything about it now. It had been too late after the first few metres. There was no going back and saying he was sorry. That would go down like a lead balloon. Overcome by a sudden burst of self-pity at the idiocy of the whole thing, he banged his handcuffs against the rock in the hope of dislodging the ratchet—but it only made them tighter still.

Running away when he'd first seen the car headlights was one thing—a not unnatural reaction—he could have pleaded he didn't realise he was dealing with the police. Escaping from custody was something else again. They would throw the book at him. It sounded bad enough sitting in the middle of a field in the early hours of the morning, but read out in court in the cold light of day, or plastered over the front page of a *journal*, it could mean the end of everything.

He tried to remember what the *gendarmes* had said. It was unlikely that they would have linked him with the banquet, if they even knew of its existence. They probably thought he'd been to a fancy dress party, or perhaps they'd assumed he was one of the singers from the Opera House suffering from overindulgence following an after-the-show party. It wouldn't take them long to discover the truth. Or would it? It depended how seriously they took the matter, or what else came up. He had a feeling the senior of the two gendarmes wouldn't rest until he'd got to the bottom of the matter.

One thing was certain. Sitting on his backside would get him nowhere. At all costs he must return to the hotel as quickly as possible. Once daylight came, discovery would be only a matter of time. He made one last effort to free himself, but it was hopeless. The handcuffs were on the last possible notch—they were biting into the flesh. In doing them up behind his back the gendarmes had known a thing or two. At least they hadn't bothered to double-lock them. In any other circumstances he could have freed himself in a matter of seconds with the aid of a piece of bent wire. It was a simple matter of lifting the ratchet wheel away from the bar. If he had a piece of bent wire!

What he needed most of all was a telephone. Making use of it with his hands behind his back would be something else again, but he would cross that bridge when he came to it. He felt tempted to give a shout—just one—in the hope that Pommes Frites might hear. But that would be tempting providence.

Everything seemed to have gone remarkably quiet. At least it wasn't raining. The sky was inky black and full of stars. He heard a twig snap somewhere close by. It was followed by a grunting noise, then silence as whatever was responsible stopped in its tracks. Conscious that something unseen was probably watching him, Monsieur Pamplemousse gave a shiver. The cold air was beginning to penetrate his costume.

He wondered what the real d'Artagnan would have done. For a start he would more than likely have been wearing the then equivalent of thermal underwear. He certainly wouldn't have been without his horse. Ever resourceful, had he lived in the present age he would doubtless have had a portable telephone tucked away somewhere as well.

Clambering to his feet, Monsieur Pamplemousse went on his way. After about a quarter of an hour he saw what he was looking for. Showing up against the skyline were two sets of cables. The first looked like a power line. The second had to be a telephone. Tossing a mental coin as to which way to go, he followed the line of posts up the side of a hill towards a small patch of woodland. Sure enough, when he came out on the other side of the trees he stumbled across a narrow track. The surface looked well worn from frequent use, and at the end of it there was a cluster of farm buildings.

Hopes raised, he made his way towards an iron gate. As he drew near a dog barked a warning. It was quickly taken up by a second animal. He waited for a moment or two, expecting to hear the sound of pounding feet, but they must have been tied up somewhere, for it didn't materialise. He heard an upper window being flung open and a shout. At least whoever lived there was already awake.

As Monsieur Pamplemousse reached the main building he backed up to the front door and thumped on it with his fists, then turned and stepped back a pace to see if it had any effect. Out of the corner of his eye he sensed a movement from one of the attic windows. Some curtains parted and he had a brief glimpse of three faces peering out at him. He assumed they must be the daughters of the house, for they were all young and patently female. Essaying a wave, he nearly fell over in the attempt, but before any of them had a chance to respond they were pushed to one side and another figure appeared. A double-barrelled shot-gun gleamed momentarily in the moonlight, then the curtains fell back into place.

He had almost given up waiting when he heard the sound of a bolt being withdrawn on the other side of the door, then another. It was followed by the metallic click of a gun being cocked.

As the door slowly opened he braced himself. '*Monsieur* . . . please forgive me for waking you at such an hour. I fear I have had an accident with my horse. I wonder if I might use your telephone?'

'You leave my daughters alone. I saw you waving at them.' The speaker had an accent you could have cut with a knife. Only a very dim light came from inside the house, but from the colour of the man's skin he guessed he was dealing with a North African, although what an Arab was doing ensconced on a hillside in the Auvergne goodness only knew. It was no moment to enquire.

'I assure you, *Monsieur*. I only wish to use your telephone.'

'That's what they all say.'

'*S'il vous plaît, Monsieur*? I will not be ungenerous.' The man peered out at him as though making a swift evaluation of his worth. 'How much?'

Monsieur Pamplemousse hesitated, thinking once again of his P.39s. Unexpected expenses were starting to mount. It was hard to say how much Madame Grante might consider reasonable in the circumstances.

Inspiration struck as he remembered he was still clutching Mrs Van Dorman's purse. Struggling as best he could to avoid letting the man see the handcuffs, he made a half turn and waved it to and fro. 'Let us just say "whatever you think is right and proper".'

The man thought it over for a moment or two. 'Where are you from?'

'Gascony.' It was as good a place as any and it seemed to satisfy the other, for he stood back and motioned with the shot-gun for Monsieur Pamplemousse to enter.

'All right, then. Just one call. But no wanting funny business afterwards.'

'*Vous êtes très gentil, Monsieur.*'

As he entered the house Monsieur Pamplemousse was greeted by a smell of stale air. It was so overpowering he wanted to reach for his handkerchief. Stale food, unwashed bodies, cheap perfume, cats; a public health inspector would have had a field day. Halfway across the room he tripped over something. It felt like a ball and chain.

There was no sign of the other occupants of the house. Everything had gone deathly quiet again. If he hadn't seen them with his own eyes they might not have existed.

'Any funny business and I'll have your *couilles* off and fry them in batter for *déjeuner*.' There was a cackle from halfway up the stairs. He groped his way towards it.

'It wouldn't be the first time,' said the voice.

'Nor the last.'

Monsieur Pamplemousse was glad when they reached the landing. The conversation was getting both one-sided and tedious. Nor did he much care for the gratuitous sound effects which accompanied the remarks.

He stood waiting while the man unlocked a door and then motioned him to enter. There was no doubt about it; he was *un bicot; un bicot* of the very worst kind. He should have stayed in North Africa where he belonged.

'In here. And don't take too long about it.'

Anxious to get the matter over with, Monsieur Pamplemousse did as he was told. The room was in darkness and as he stood waiting for his eyes to get accustomed to the gloom the door slammed shut behind him.

'*Merde!*' It was the second time that evening he'd been caught unawares. He made a dive for the door, but before he was halfway there he heard the sound of a key being turned.

'*Bougnoule! Melon!* Come back! Let me out!'

The only response was another cackle.

In desperation Monsieur Pamplemousse delivered

a kick in the direction of the sound, then immediately regretted it as he made contact with the door.

Having felt in vain for a light switch and drawn a blank, he hobbled across to the window and looked out. Any hope of making a jump for it faded fast. Immediately below him there was a pile of old farm implements. Monsieur Pamplemousse didn't fancy his chances if he landed on them. The old man's wishes might be granted sooner than he expected. Even in the moonlight their barbs and prongs looked lethal.

Seeing everything from a different angle showed that he was in some kind of scrap-yard. Pieces of rusty farm machinery lay everywhere. Most of it looked as though it had been there for years. An old open-topped bus stood in one corner, its chassis broken. Weeds sprouted from unlikely places. Somewhat surprisingly there was a tarmac area which seemed to have been set aside for a makeshift car park. There were lines painted on it to mark the spaces, but there was no sign of a car.

Somewhere amongst it all there had to be a ladder, or at least something that would serve as one. If only he could get at it. He turned away from the window hoping there might at least be a bed with some sheets, but the room seemed totally devoid of furniture. He couldn't even find anywhere to sit.

Monsieur Pamplemousse spent the next ten minutes or so pacing up and down in a state of growing frustration. After a while he thought he detected a noise coming from the corridor. He crept towards the door and put his ear to it. He could hear someone whispering. It was followed by a giggle.

'*Qui est là?*' At the sound of his voice the noise stopped abruptly.

He tried again. 'Who is there? Can you open the door?'

'No. It is not possible. He has the key.' The voice was female; the accent a softer version of the man's.

'In that case, we have an *impasse*.' Nice though it was to hear another voice, there seemed little point in pursuing the conversation.

A piece of paper appeared under the door. It was followed by more giggles. Crouching down, Monsieur Pamplemousse managed to pick it up. He took it across to the window, placed it on the sill, then turned and peered at it. He could hardly believe his eyes. Expecting a message of some kind, he was confronted instead with a coloured drawing.

'*Sacré bleu!*' He couldn't help himself. Even without the aid of a torch it was clear that anatomically correct though the result might be, its influences owed more to readings of the Kama Sutra than from any medical publication. Explicit was hardly the word. *Extraordinaire* was more like it.

In a fit of desperation Monsieur Pamplemousse opened Mrs Van Dorman's purse and felt inside it. There was a small comb, a handkerchief, several articles he couldn't immediately identify, and then . . . he found what he was looking for. Undoing the top of a lipstick he put the holder in his mouth, turned the paper over, and began laboriously writing out a message.

MY HANDS ARE TIED. PLEASE FREE ME. I WILL PAY YOU WELL. NAME YOUR PRICE.

His task completed, he passed it under the door and waited for some kind of reaction. His only reward was another burst of giggling.

He was about to remonstrate when a dog barked. The others must have heard it too, for without another word they disappeared down the corridor. Once again there was a shout followed by silence.

Peering through the open window he made out the familiar shape of Pommes Frites crouched in a patch of weeds on the far side. Pommes Frites was much too well trained to give any sign that he had seen his master, but he gradually eased his way across the yard on his stomach until he reached the pile of machinery below the window where he waited, his tail moving gently to and fro.

Monsieur Pamplemousse allowed himself to be seen for a brief moment, then threw Mrs Van Dorman's purse down to him. Pommes Frites sniffed it once. The message was clear without his master having to utter so much as a word.

Once again, as had so often happened in the past, it was a case of *cherchez la femme*.

Following a trail carefully laid at strategic points on the outward journey, Pommes Frites set off into the darkness, glad that at long last there was something concrete to do.

Monsieur Pamplemousse watched until he had disappeared from view. It would be some while before he would see Pommes Frites again, but that he would see him before the night was over he had little doubt.

He wondered if the recipients of his note were making equal efforts on his behalf. Somehow, he doubted it. Perhaps all three were tucked up in bed hard at work on more drawings.

Unable to check the hour by virtue of a handicap which Messrs Cupillard Rième could scarcely have been expected to foresee when they designed the dial of his wrist watch, Monsieur Pamplemousse sat down to wait, counting off in his mind first the seconds, then the minutes.

As an exercise in passing the time it soon began to pall, and he had long since given up making the effort when he heard the sound of an engine. And not just any old engine; it was the unmistakable noise made by the 602cc flat-twin, air-cooled engine of a Citroën *deux chevaux*.

It stopped some distance away and then there was silence again. Mrs Van Dorman was learning fast. Straining his eyes for any sign of movement, Monsieur Pamplemousse stationed himself by the open window. Doubtless Pommes Frites would lead the way; and what was perhaps even more important, it would be done quietly and stealthily so as to avoid waking any of the others. He would be in his element. With luck, there wouldn't be much longer to wait.

6

COMINGS AND GOINGS

MONSIEUR PAMPLEMOUSSE LAY BACK ON THE BED, too tired even to remove the sword dangling from his belt. Closing his eyes for a moment, he concentrated all his energies on fighting off a growing feeling of claustrophobia at still having his hands securely fastened behind his back. Never before had he felt quite so powerless, or so frustrated.

'Are you sure you have nothing?' he called. 'No safety-pins? Not even a paper-clip?'

'I have pins galore.' Mrs Van Dorman searched through a tray on her dressing table. 'Long ones, short ones, fat ones, thin ones . . . you name it. I just don't have anything I can use to make a right angle bend in one.'

'*Merde!*' If only he'd been in his own room. If he'd been in his own room he would have had his emergency case—the one issued by *Le Guide*; designed to cater for all eventualities. The possibility of having to bend the end of a safety-pin or a piece of stiff wire in order to break open a set of handcuffs, although not specifically envisaged in the list of basic requirements, would have been *pas de problème*. One twist with the small pair of pliers included in his wisdom by the founder, and he would have been home and dry.

'Poor Aristide. Are you feeling very frustrated?'

Monsieur Pamplemousse opened his eyes and raised them ceiling-wards as he felt a tug, first on his right leg, then on his left. It was a self-answering question.

Mrs Van Dorman slid his boots under the bed. 'What are you thinking?'

'I was thinking that you are very kind. I don't know what I would have done tonight without you. If it wasn't for you I would still be incarcerated in that dreadful farmhouse.' In truth he was thinking many other things as well. His mind was awash with thoughts.

'What else? You are very quiet.'

'I was wondering about Pommes Frites' sense of smell. I am a little worried that he may be losing it.'

'How can you say that after all he's been through? He followed you to the farmhouse, then back here. Then he led me all the way back to the farmhouse again while I drove the car. Listen to him . . . poor thing . . . he's quite worn out.'

Almost as though he was aware in his sleep that he was being talked about, Pommes Frites gave a loud snore. It was the first of many to come.

Monsieur Pamplemousse was less than sympathetic. 'Following me there the first time was second nature; that is what he is trained to do. Going back to it again was simply a matter of covering old ground. As for finding his way to the hotel between whiles—he has his methods. After all the *asperge* he ate earlier in the evening he could hardly have gone wrong. No, it was something else which makes me wonder. As you say, his nose cannot be entirely redundant, but I wonder if it is only firing on three cylinders.'

'I think we probably all are at the moment.' Mrs Van Dorman plumped up his pillow. 'And what else do we have on our mind?'

'I was thinking I must send a fax message.'

'Now? Right this minute? Can't it wait until morning?'

'The sooner the better. In Paris I have a set of skeleton keys.'

'How do you know one of them will fit?'

'It will. All I have to do is match a key to the make. The mechanism is really very basic. In most cases one key will fit all locks from the same manufacturer.' Given time he was sure he could instruct Mrs Van Dorman in the ancient art of lock-picking, but to have a set of keys would be an insurance policy in the event that he failed. For all he knew she might be totally impractical; unable to open a can of soup, let alone a pair of *menottes*.

It would have sounded ungracious to add that for the moment at least he wanted nothing more than to be left alone with his thoughts. He was at a stage when normally he would have made a list of questions that needed answering. If he'd had his notebook . . . and if he'd been in a position to hold a pen. He let out a sigh. There were so many 'if's'.

'OK.' Mrs Van Dorman took the hint. 'Tell me what you want to say. I'll see if I can wake the night clerk.

123

If he's not around I'll send it myself. Where do you want it to go?'

'It is to my office.' Monsieur Pamplemousse gave her the number, then dictated as succinct a message as possible. 'Mark it for the attention of the Director's secretary—Véronique. She will know what to do.'

As the door closed behind Mrs Van Dorman, he tried to get out of bed, but after a moment or two gave up the struggle. His whole body was aching. It felt as though no part of it had gone unscathed from the ride on the horse. Bits that he didn't know existed were making their presence felt. He glanced at a clock on the bedside table. It was after three o'clock. Alongside the clock was an open box of fudge. It was nice to think of Mrs Van Dorman having a guilty secret.

Monsieur Pamplemousse lay back and closed his eyes again. Beginning at the beginning, he started running through the various questions uppermost in his mind.

That Norm's demise had cast little more than a passing shadow on the previous night's proceedings was patently obvious, but he couldn't help feeling there was some other element involved.

There was the question of Spencer Troon's performance over dinner for a start; pretending he'd been poisoned. That it hadn't exactly endeared him to Elliott was hardly surprising in the circumstances. But what had been behind Spencer's remark that at least it made him 'runner-up'? Runner-up to what? Or to whom?

And then there was Pommes Frites' strange behaviour, which had occasioned his remark to Mrs Van Dorman. Why had he ignored her glass of wine when it was knocked over? He hadn't given it so much as a

124

passing sniff, treating it almost with contempt. And yet there definitely had been a scent of bitter almonds, reminiscent of the smell they had both received from Ellis's tasting glass. If he, Pamplemousse, had noticed it, why hadn't Pommes Frites? Normally he would have been in there like a shot.

His thoughts were broken into at that point by the return of Mrs Van Dorman. She looked flushed as she let herself into the room, opening and closing the door as quietly as possible.

She put a finger to her lips. 'The *gendarme* is still outside your room. I think you'd better stay here for the time being.'

Monsieur Pamplemousse didn't feel disposed to argue.

'Let me cover you up—you'll get cold.' Mrs Van Dorman pulled the eiderdown up over him. 'There's nothing else we can do until morning. The fax has gone off. And I had a word with the night clerk. I've asked him to arrange with the telephonist tomorrow morning to have any calls for you transferred to this room.'

'You think he will oblige?'

'I'm sure he will if he wants to earn the rest of his bonus. Besides, the whole place reeks of nepotism. The bell captain is his uncle, and the switchboard operator just happens to be the granddaughter of a friend. He's promised to pass the word around to the rest of the staff. I get the feeling he doesn't like the police.'

Monsieur Pamplemousse nodded. It was probably an echo of some unmentionable wrong dating back to the war years. The police must have gained a lot of enemies in Vichy during the time the pro-Hitler puppet government was in residence.

'How about the man outside my door? Do you think he heard you coming up in the lift?'

'No way. I used the back stairs.'

The thought of Mrs Van Dorman bothering to come up the back stairs on his behalf made Monsieur Pamplemousse feel strangely excited. What was the old saying? The most beautiful moment of a love affair is the one when you are climbing the stairs. Even if the sentiment were true, it didn't seem like a moment they were destined to share.

Mrs Van Dorman hovered for a moment. 'Do you mind if I have a quick shower? I'm dying to get out of these clothes. I've been corseted long enough.'

'Of course not.'

Monsieur Pamplemousse wondered if he should take her into his confidence. Obviously the whole thing was giving her a kind of vicarious pleasure, but he was reluctant to give voice to thoughts that were still only half formed in his own mind, and the sound of running water put paid for the time being to any hope of conversation.

He had to hand it to her. Not once during the drive back had she questioned his behaviour. Not once had she asked him about his encounter with the police. Nor had she hesitated for a moment, as some women might have done, when she learned they were awaiting his arrival back at the hotel. Rather the reverse; clearly it had set the adrenalin flowing.

Grudgingly, Monsieur Pamplemousse took his hat off to the locals. They had got on to him far quicker than he'd expected them to.

Wriggling his hands behind his belt, he managed to turn it until the buckle was at the rear and he was able to grapple with the fastening. There was a clunk as belt, scabbard and sword landed on the floor. The relief was indescribable.

'Are you OK? It sounded as though you'd fallen out of bed.' Mrs Van Dorman arrived back in the bedroom. She was wearing a pair of pink silk pyjamas with bell-bottom trousers. The jacket had her initials embroidered on the pocket. The wig had gone, but the beauty spot was still in place. Perhaps she had forgotten it was there, or perhaps she felt it lent an air of abandon to the situation.

'Mind if I join you?' Without waiting for an answer she turned out the bedside light.

Monsieur Pamplemousse felt a draught of cool air overlaid with a waft of the perfume she had been using earlier in the evening. A moment later the bedclothes were in place again.

He lay silent for a while drinking in the smell of honeysuckle and jasmine. It was like a breath of blossom-time encapsulated between the sheets, refreshing and at the same time curiously disturbing.

'Now what are you thinking?'

'I was wondering, statistically, how many men there are in France at this moment dressed as d'Artagnan, in bed with a beautiful lady, their hands powerless behind their back.' Perhaps in some establishments on the foothills of Montmartre, or in rooms off the rue St Denis where they catered to bizarre tastes.

'I guess the answer would have to be pretty minimal. And not just in France.'

He sensed a hesitation in her voice. 'Anyway, you shouldn't pay compliments you don't mean.'

'But I do mean it.'

'You know something? No one has said that to me for a very long time.'

127

Monsieur Pamplemousse rolled over on his left side and immediately wished he hadn't.

'What are *you* thinking?' he asked, masking his discomfort.

'I was thinking, Aristide, you really should remove your sword when you are in bed with a lady.'

'And I feel it is only fair to warn you,' said Monsieur Pamplemousse, 'that is not cold steel you feel.'

'Oh?'

There was a slight movement beside him as she moved closer, then a moment's silence.

'Nor is it!'

'Tell me.' It was his turn to ask the questions. 'How do you think Monsieur d'Artagnan would have behaved in similar circumstances?'

'From all I have heard he wouldn't have been above asking a lady for her assistance. It is a question of where your priorities lie.'

The response came in the form of a deep sigh. 'I doubt', said Monsieur Pamplemousse, 'if he had my problem.'

Unable to contain himself a moment longer, he sat up in bed. Ever since they had set off on the journey back to the hotel, there had been one thought above all others uppermost in his mind. He had tried his best to ignore it, but it was no longer possible. The ride down from the hills had been bad enough. The sound of the shower had been the last straw.

'*Excusez moi* . . . I, too, have a priority . . . it is one which is of the utmost urgency.'

Easing himself down beneath the eiderdown, Monsieur Pamplemousse encountered a hand. He kissed it briefly, then rolled off the end of the bed.

As he groped his way round the foot and headed towards the bathroom his feet encountered something solid. Giving voice to a yelp of pain, Pommes Frites leapt to his feet and sent his master spinning in the direction of the dressing table.

As the sound of the crash echoed round the room, Mrs Van Dorman switched on the bedside light. 'Boy!', she exclaimed, taking in the scene. 'Do you ever need help!'

Monsieur Pamplemousse stirred in his sleep, gradually becoming aware that horizontal shafts of sunlight were filtering through the shutter. He opened one eye. Mrs Van Dorman's head was on the adjoining pillow, barely inches away from his own. In the half-light she looked different; almost as though there was something missing. He noticed, not for the first time, how blue her eyes were.

'*Bonjour*, Aristide.'

'*Bonjour* . . .' He wanted desperately to rub his own eyes as he tried to force himself awake.

'You went out like the proverbial light last night. It was all I could do to get you back to bed.'

It was true. He hardly remembered a thing. The combination of the food and the wine and all that followed, had acted like a 'knock-out' drop. For the second night running he had slept like a log.

'What is the time now?'

'Almost twelve o'clock.'

'*Morbleu!*'

'I don't plan on going anywhere, Aristide,' said Mrs Van Dorman. 'Do you?'

Monsieur Pamplemousse felt the handcuffs biting into his wrists. His arms were like lead weights. 'I couldn't go anywhere,' he said ruefully, 'even if I wanted to.'

There was a stirring from somewhere nearby as

129

Pommes Frites stood up and shook himself awake at the sound of voices. A face appeared over the end of the bed. Monsieur Pamplemousse recognised the signs; the doleful look, the chin resting on the cover, the soulful eyes gazing up at the ceiling. An artist searching for models to illustrate a series of paintings based on well-known phrases would have needed to look no further when he came to 'hang-dog expression'. No doubt Pommes Frites would be making his way towards the door at any moment, pointedly asking for his morning stroll; he was no respecter of moments.

'DiAnn . . .'

'You can call me Dee if you like. Most of my friends do.'

'Dee . . .' It felt strange enough using her Christian name, let alone in a truncated form. 'May I ask you something?'

'Go ahead . . .'

Monsieur Pamplemousse hesitated as he heard settling down noises. Perhaps Pommes Frites' instincts were telling him to build up his reserves again. After all his activity during the night they could probably do with replenishment.

A moment later the subject was driven from his mind as the telephone rang. The sound was so loud and unexpected he nearly fell out of bed.

'I guess that's another problem d'Artagnan wouldn't have had to face.' Mrs Van Dorman sounded resigned.

'If we ignore it, perhaps it will go away.'

Monsieur Pamplemousse reckoned without Pommes Frites. Ever alive to his master's needs, he rose to his feet again and padded round the side of the bed. As far as he was concerned there was too much talk and too little action. The sooner the talking was over and done with and he could go out for a walk the better.

Something hard and wet landed on the pillow beside Monsieur Pamplemousse's head. As it did so a familiar voice issued from one end.

'Pamplemousse! What *is* going on? Are you there?' The Director's voice came through loud and clear.

'*Oui, Monsieur.* I am here.'

He exchanged a glance with Mrs Van Dorman. It mirrored that worn by Pommes Frites a moment earlier.

'Pamplemousse, you must remain exactly where you are. Do not move.'

'*Oui, Monsieur.* I shall be most happy to oblige.'

Mrs Van Dorman tried, not entirely successfully, to smother a giggle.

'Pamplemousse ... did I hear another voice just then? Do I take it you are not on your own?'

Monsieur Pamplemousse parried the question. 'Possibly it was a crossed line, *Monsieur.*'

'Hmm.' The Director didn't sound entirely convinced. Fortunately, he clearly had other things on his mind.

'Pamplemousse, how long have you been in Vichy?'

'Two days, *Monsieur.*'

'Two days, Pamplemousse, and two *nights*! I put you in charge, and what happens?

'One of America's foremost gastronomic magazine publishers goes missing, two *gendarmes* have been attacked, three maidens ravished, the police forces of four continents are on the look-out for you, and *Le Cercle de Six* has become *Le Cercle de Cinq*. It is no wonder you are on the run from the authorities.'

Monsieur Pamplemousse stirred uneasily. The Director made it sound like a new arrangement with variations for words and music of 'The Twelve Days of Christmas'.

'What is wrong, Pamplemousse? Are you listening?'

'*Oui, Monsieur.* It is simply that I am lying with my left ear on the telephone receiver and it is very painful.'

In the few moments it took the Director to absorb the information, Monsieur Pamplemousse managed to adjust to a more comfortable position.

'May I ask, Pamplemousse, what is wrong with your right ear? Do you have to use your left?'

'It is difficult to explain, *Monsieur*, but the simple answer is *"oui, c'est très necessaire"*. I am sore from all that has happened. Turning is difficult.'

'In view of the reports I have received concerning your activities over the past twenty-four hours I am not surprised.'

'It is not what you think, *Monsieur*. It is mostly from the horse.'

'When I arranged for you to have a *cheval*, Pamplemousse, I did not expect you to use it in order to live the part of d'Artagnan to the full—roaming the countryside, terrorising the local populace, pillaging and raping, *gauche, droit et centre*.

'It would have been better if I had sent you to the banquet dressed as *Henry V*—a prince known to all and sundry as *Le Vert galant*. If my memory serves me correctly, he was awarded the title on account of his excessive sexual activities; activities which remained undiminished until he met his death at the hands of an assassin. Had he been alive today he would have had to look to his laurels, lest he forfeit the title.

'A warrant has been issued for your arrest. Interpol

has been alerted. All manner of crimes have been laid at your doorstep; crimes culled from files which have been gathering dust over the past decade. Years of unsolved cases are beginning to surface. Everything from attempted rape in Yugoslavia to fire-raising in Provence. Fortunately, the description they have of you is somewhat hazy. I suggest you either remove your beard at the earliest opportunity or have it dyed another colour.'

Monsieur Pamplemousse settled back. The Director had the bit well and truly between his teeth. He could be in for a long session.

'There is absolutely nothing they can charge me with, *Monsieur*. I may have run away from the police, but who wouldn't at that hour in the morning on a lonely country road? How was I to know they were who they said they were. They produced no form of identity.'

'*Ortolans*, Pamplemousse. *Ortolans*. Aiding and abetting in the cooking and eating of *ortolans*—a serious offence.'

'*Ortolans, Monsieur*? But I did not know . . .'

'I'm sure you don't need to be reminded, Pamplemousse, that ignorance of the law is no excuse in the eyes of the authorities. I must admit I was unaware of a change in the regulations myself, but due to over-indulgence—mostly in the area of the Landes—the EEC in their wisdom have deemed *ortolans* to be a protected species, along with fig-pickers and the Pyrenean Brown bear.'

Monsieur Pamplemousse hardly listened. It was true. If they wanted to they could get you on anything. If it hadn't been *ortolans* it would have been something else—like stealing the handcuffs. It was one of the first things he had learned in the force. If all else failed, accidentally push them over and charge them with resisting arrest.

'I wish to goodness I had never got involved in this whole thing,' continued the Director. 'We shall be the laughing stock of France if it ever emerges that one of our staff has indulged in nefarious culinary practices.'

'It was hardly my fault, *Monsieur*.' Monsieur Pamplemousse felt obliged to protest. 'I did not devise the menu.' He felt Mrs Van Dorman nodding her head vigorously in agreement. 'Besides, for all anyone knows I might not even have touched the *ortolans*. My conscience could well have forbidden it. The evidence is all circumstantial.'

'That is as may be, Aristide, but it was Thoreau, was it not, who said "Some circumstantial evidence is very strong—as when you find a trout in the milk"?'

'With all due respect to Thoreau, *Monsieur*, he did not have to stand up in court and explain to the good burghers of Vichy how he happened to be knocking on the door of a lonely farmhouse in the early hours of the morning dressed as d'Artagnan.'

'Ah,' broke in the Director. 'I am glad you mention that, Pamplemousse. It brings me to the matter of the three maidens. How you came to be there in the first place is beyond me, but the fact remains that notes were sent. Money was proffered. An obscene drawing is to be exhibit "A". An obscene drawing passed during the hours of darkness to three innocent creatures.'

'One note, *Monsieur*, and no money exchanged hands. The "obscene drawing" as you put it, happened to be on the back of the note. As for their innocence, that is something I am unable to comment on since I only caught a brief glimpse of their faces at an upper window.'

'I hardly think that is a good defence, Pamplemousse. You were the one who pushed the note under the door in the first place. There are three witnesses who are willing to swear to it.'

'Not in the first place, *Monsieur*. In the second. They pushed it under the door to me first.'

'It is your word against theirs, Pamplemousse. One against three.'

'Are you saying you do not believe me, *Monsieur*?'

'No, Pamplemousse, I am not saying that. What I choose to believe or disbelieve is really immaterial. What matters is what those in court believe. I do not fancy your chances. The evidence against you is overwhelming. The wording of the note, "MY HANDS ARE TIED. PLEASE FREE ME. I WILL PAY YOU WELL. NAME YOUR PRICE," speaks volumes. They are words which will be hard to explain if you are confronted by a skilled interlocutor.'

Monsieur Pamplemousse drew a deep breath and prepared to play his trump card. 'It will need a very skilled interlocutor indeed, *Monsieur*, to demonstrate in court precisely how I was able to execute a drawing in such great and explicit detail while my hands were tightly secured behind my back.'

The silence gave him much-needed breathing space. Arguments with the Director always left him feeling drained. He stole a glance at Mrs Van Dorman. It struck him that she was looking unusually thoughtful.

'You say your hands were secured *behind* your back?'

'*Oui, Monsieur*. With a pair of *menottes*.'

'Ah, I see your dilemma. So you did not climb into bed with intent to ravish these girls as their father maintains.'

'No, *Monsieur*. I did not. I did not even see their

135

bed, for the very simple reason that I was locked inside another room. A room from which I have since escaped. Furthermore, *Monsieur*, my hands are still cuffed together. Short of cutting the jacket free, I cannot even undress . . .'

'Cut your jacket free!' The Director reacted in horror at the thought. 'I trust you will do no such thing, Aristide. It was hired at great expense. I cannot begin to tell you the trouble I experienced clearing the bill with Madame Grante in the first place. If it is damaged in any way I shall never hear the last of it. Nor, I fear, will you.'

'In that case, *Monsieur*, perhaps you would be kind enough to suggest an alternative.'

'Can you not telephone Glandier? If he is as good a magician as you say he is, I am sure he will know of a method of removing a jacket without undoing the *menottes*. It is the kind of thing one has seen done many times on the stage.'

Monsieur Pamplemousse relaxed. Having let off steam, the Director was obviously going off the boil. Now it was his turn. 'I'm sure you are right in what you say, *Monsieur*. It would not do to appear in court alongside you wearing a jacket which has been ripped apart from top to bottom, the lining protruding . . .'

'Alongside me, Pamplemousse?'

'I assume you will be speaking on my behalf, *Monsieur*. After all, the whole enterprise was your idea. I am only here as your representative.'

The Director sounded dubious. 'I will, of course, engage a good lawyer to act on your behalf. That is the least I can do. But as for appearing myself, I am not sure that would be wise. The adverse publicity . . .' He paused for thought. 'I shall have to await progress reports before I make a decision.'

'You shall have one, *Monsieur*, just as soon as my hands are free. I am working on the case. But if you would rather I didn't, I can always make a clean breast of things. Before going to the police I could telephone the local *journal* and try to enlist their sympathy. No doubt they would welcome an article on the banquet . . .'

It had the desired effect.

'Don't misunderstand me, Aristide. Of course I don't want you to stop what you are doing. I value your judgement in these matters. And if anyone is to receive the benefit of an article I trust it will be the Staff magazine. I shall look forward to seeing the photographs as well in due course, but in the meantime . . .'

'In the meantime, *Monsieur*, in certain areas I have made a good deal of progress. *Par exemple*, I know the exact whereabouts of Mrs Van Dorman . . .'

'You do? Good work, Aristide! This is *incroyable*. When news started filtering through during the early hours of this morning I tried to telephone her. I was told she was not in her room. Naturally I assumed the worst . . .'

'She is safe and well, *Monsieur*.'

'But where is she? Tell me. You must bring her back to Paris at once.'

'I am afraid that is not possible, *Monsieur*.'

'Not possible?'

'There are things I must do before I leave Vichy. I need to satisfy my curiosity over certain matters.'

Out of the corner of his eye he saw Mrs Van Dorman nodding vigorously.

'Besides, I have to wait until the postman arrives.'

'Ah!' The Director sounded more cheerful. 'Now there *I* have good news for you, Pamplemousse. If

137

you are referring to your fax message about the keys, the night staff alerted Véronique and she came into the office early this morning. She has already taken the necessary action and she assures me they will be with you shortly.

'As for my being with you, I will do my best to slot you in. However, as you know, the new edition of *Le Guide* has not long been out and it is always a busy period. In the meantime I will get on to my good friend the Deputy again. I'm sure he will do his best, but in order to pull strings one first has to find the right ends and it is not his region . . .'

'*Oui, Monsieur.*' Monsieur Pamplemousse allowed the Director sufficient time to justify to his own satisfaction the many reasons why he might not be able to make the journey to Vichy, then uttered his '*aux revoirs*' and signalled Mrs Van Dorman to cut the call. There was a click as the line went dead.

As she stretched across him to replace the receiver in its cradle, he lay back exhausted.

It was a moment or two before either of them spoke.

'You know, Aristide,' said Mrs Van Dorman. 'You are the only man I've ever kissed whose beard tasted of glue.'

'You have kissed many men with beards?' asked Monsieur Pamplemousse.

'Come to think of it, no. Come to think of it, you're the very first.'

'Perhaps it is a fact of life that all men's beards taste of glue.'

'I'll let you know. You've given me a taste for it. I'll tell you something else. When you kissed me back I heard the proverbial bell ringing.'

'I heard it too,' said Monsieur Pamplemousse. 'I am afraid I can still hear it. It is very persistent.'

'Maybe you'd better take the call,' said Mrs Van Dorman. 'I don't think it's going away.'

Reaching across for the receiver again, she held it against his ear, brushing her lips across his forehead as she did so. Pommes Frites, who had been on his way to render service, assumed his resigned 'here we go again' expression and went back to bed.

The voice, when it emerged was even more familiar than the first. Monsieur Pamplemousse's heart sank.

'*Couscous!* How wonderful.' He made faces at Mrs Van Dorman. 'And how clear your voice is. You could be right here in Vichy.'

'I *am* in Vichy, Aristide. I am waiting for someone to show me up to your room. For some reason the staff seem very reluctant to do so.'

In a sudden panic, Monsieur Pamplemousse pressed his head against the mouthpiece. '*Merde!*' he hissed. 'It is my wife—Madame Pamplemousse. She is here. In Vichy!'

'Jesus!' Mrs Van Dorman was out of bed like a shot.

'I am sorry, *chèrie*. What was that you said?'

'I said why are you covering the mouthpiece, Aristide? Is there someone else with you? If it is another chambermaid . . .'

'*Couscous.* I promise you . . . on my honour. Have you *seen* the chambermaid. She is old enough to be my mother . . .'

'That did not seem to bother you in La Rochelle.'

'Once and for all, Doucette . . .' Playing for time, Monsieur Pamplemousse watched helplessly while Mrs Van Dorman swept as many of her belongings as she could into a case and bundled it into the wardrobe. 'La Rochelle is not what you think it was. If only

139

you wouldn't jump to conclusions. I can explain everything . . .' He suddenly realised the receiver had gone dead and he was talking to himself.

'Quick, she must be on her way.' Even as he spoke he heard the faint sound of lift doors opening and closing.

Mrs Van Dorman dived into the cupboard. She wasn't a moment too soon. As the door swung shut behind her, the one leading to the corridor opened and the porter peered nervously round the corner.

'*Monsieur . . .*'

'*Entrez. Entrez.*' Monsieur Pamplemousse did his best to keep the note of impending doom from his voice. '*Couscous*, what a wonderful surprise!'

Doucette look round suspiciously as she followed the porter into the room. 'Why are the shutters still drawn, Aristide? Do you know what time it is? I have been up since dawn. The train left Paris at eight forty-three.'

'And I', said Monsieur Pamplemousse virtuously, 'have hardly *fermé les yeux* all night.'

'*Monsieur?*' Hovering nervously on the sidelines, the porter gestured towards the window.

'Please do. It is time I was up.'

As the man slowly and laboriously wound up the shutter and the room was flooded with light, Monsieur Pamplemousse took a quick glance at his surroundings. He breathed an inward sigh of relief. Mrs Van Dorman had done a good job. As far as he could tell there was nothing untoward in view. Nothing that he couldn't talk his way out of.

The porter looked equally relieved as he made good his escape. He was probably worried about his bonus.

As soon as they were on their own Doucette flung

open the balcony doors. 'This room smells like a brothel.'

Monsieur Pamplemousse resisted the temptation to ask how she knew. It was no time for scoring cheap points.

'Do you have the keys?'

Rummaging in her capacious handbag, Doucette found what she was looking for. 'Are these the ones? They were in the bureau drawer.'

Spreading them out on the bedcover, she waited while Monsieur Pamplemousse glanced through them.

'How on earth did this happen—to you of all people?'

'It is a long story . . .'

'An Inspector in the Paris Sûreté.'

'Ex,' said Monsieur Pamplemousse.

'I'm not surprised.'

Monsieur Pamplemousse chose to ignore the last remark. 'Try the small one next to the Yale. That should do it.'

Rolling over on to his side he waited patiently for Doucette to undo the first lock. As she bent over him she paused and gave a sniff. 'What is that scent?'

'Scent?' repeated Monsieur Pamplemousse.

'Ah, *oui*, the scent. It is of the period. I wore it at the banquet last night. I resisted the idea at first, but the costumiers insisted. In those days many men of a certain class wore perfume. It was said to be a particular favourite of Louis XIV. That is why they called him the "Sweet-smelling Monarch". It is made from the petals of jasmine and honeysuckle. If you like it, *chèrie*, I will buy you some when I get back to Paris. It is from Jean Laporte.'

'You have become very expert at perfume all of a sudden,' said Doucette suspiciously.

Monsieur Pamplemousse broke off in mid-flight. She was right, of course. He mustn't overdo it. There was nothing more incriminating than being over-enthusiastic. How often had he not witnessed the same thing in the old days when he was questioning a suspect; a sudden burst of eloquence over some trivial matter in the hope of diverting attention. Apart from which, now that the moment was so near, he could hardly wait to be released.

'Hurry, *Couscous*.'

He waited impatiently while his wife fiddled with the keys.

'It is difficult with so many. The others get in the way.'

A moment later his hands were free. The relief was indescribable. For a second or two his shoulders felt so stiff he could hardly move, let alone bring his arms round in front of him, but at last he managed it. Taking the bunch of keys from Doucette, he undid the second lock.

'Your poor wrists. They are almost raw.' She leant forward to embrace him. 'I shall stay and look after you until they are better.'

Monsieur Pamplemousse stopped rubbing himself immediately. 'That is not necessary, *chèrie*. In a matter of a few hours they will be as right as rain again. It is only a little redness . . .' He broke off as he realised Doucette was hardly listening. Instead, she was staring in horror at something behind his left shoulder.

'What is wrong, *Couscous*?' he asked nervously.

'Aristide! There is something on the other pillow. Something round and black.'

Turning his head, Monsieur Pamplemousse followed the direction of his wife's gaze. His heart nearly missed a beat. There, on the pillow, was Mrs Van Dorman's beauty spot. It must have fallen off during the night. No wonder she had looked different in the morning.

'Voilà!'

Regardless of the pain in his wrists, he made as though to swat the object. As he did so he managed to scoop it up in his fingers. In desperation he handed it to Pommes Frites, who was also giving the matter his undivided attention. Pommes Frites' gratitude at receiving his master's benefaction was short lived. Pleasurable chomping noises gave way almost at once to violent choking. It sounded as though he might be having trouble with a tooth. Either that or the object had stuck to the back of his throat.

'Poor thing,' said Doucette. 'What do you think it could have been?'

'A bed bug of some kind.' Monsieur Pamplemousse dismissed the matter as hardly worthy of discussion.

'But it looked enormous. I have never seen such a big one.'

'Doubtless it became bloated through feeding on me all through the night,' said Monsieur Pamplemousse. He wriggled inside his costume. 'This hotel is full of such creatures. It is disgraceful. I feel itchy all over.'

Taking his cue, Pommes Frites, who had been listening to the conversation with growing concern, put two and two together on his master's behalf. Pausing in his retching, he began scratching himself vigorously. He looked a sorry sight.

Doucette reached for her handbag. 'If that is the

143

case, I am certainly *not* staying here a moment longer.'

'Are you sure, *Couscous*? Is there nothing I can say to make you change your mind?'

Madame Pamplemousse wriggled. 'Indeed not.' She cast a disapproving eye around the room. 'I am surprised you even suggest it. *And* I shall tell them at the desk exactly why I am not staying.'

'I would rather you didn't, *Couscous*. Not before I make out a report to Headquarters.'

'I think the sooner you get back to Paris and submit it the better.'

Monsieur Pamplemousse gave a sigh. 'I know you sometimes think life is all champagne and roses when I am away, Doucette, but as you see . . .' He gave the pillow a thump and immediately wished he hadn't. Apart from a searing pain which shot up his right arm, the blow released a fresh cloud of invisible esters, filling the room with perfume as they rose into the air.

'As for the smell . . .' Madame Pamplemousse's sniff said it all. 'It's no wonder France had to suffer a revolution if that's what men went about wearing.'

'I think you will find there is a fast train at thirteen-thirty-eight.' Monsieur Pamplemousse glanced up from a plasticised information sheet on the bedside table. 'It will get you to Paris just before five o'clock. There is a restaurant car, so you will be able to have lunch. I don't wish to hurry you, but if you go now you should just catch it.'

'Are you sure?' Doucette hesitated. 'I feel as though I am deserting you.'

'Don't worry about me,' said Monsieur Pamplemousse. 'I shall be all right. Besides, I have work to do.' He raised his hands as far as the pain from the

144

slowly returning circulation would allow, then let them fall again. There was no point in overdoing the protestations.

'Your beard', said Doucette, as she kissed him goodbye, 'tastes of glue!'

Monsieur Pamplemousse listened at the door for the lift gates to close and as soon as he heard a satisfactory clang he slid a security bolt into place and turned towards the cupboard.

Opening the door, he put his head inside. The blue track suit was hanging in one corner. He recognised the outfit worn on the journey down. The dress for the banquet hung in an opposite corner. In between the two there were summer frocks and evening gowns galore.

'DiAnn! It is safe. You can come out now.'

Parting the hangers in the middle, he slid them to one side and began groping in the area behind, half expecting Mrs Van Dorman to jump out at him.

Gradually faint irritation at playing games gave way to surprise, then a sense of shock. It was hard to take in for a moment, but a second and then a third search confirmed the simple truth. To all intents and purposes both Mrs Van Dorman and her suitcase had vanished into thin air.

7

PUTTING OUT THE CREAM

GLANDIER WOULD HAVE BEEN PLEASED; IT WOULD have appealed to his sense of humour.

As a stage act, it might not have lived up to the high standards set by the great magicians of the past; illusionists of the calibre of Maskelyne and Devante, who were able to make elephants disappear before your very eyes. For a start they would have insisted on the inside of the cupboard being painted matt black, thus ensuring there would be no tell-tale reflections of light from an unpainted knob or hinge; gleams which would have revealed the existence of an old door built into the wall at the back.

'I guess I must have noticed it when I got un-packed,' said Mrs Van Dorman, 'but it didn't register. It wasn't until I hid behind the things hanging up and felt something digging into me that I thought of trying

146

the handle. Who'd have guessed it would open into the next room?'

Who indeed? It was yet another echo from the past, a throwback to the days when whole families stayed in Vichy to take the cure.

However, the simple question gave rise to a number of others. Why, for instance, had the door been unlocked in the first place? Had it always been left that way, or had someone unlocked it recently, perhaps when they entered Mrs Van Dorman's looking for Ellis's glass.

'Your wife has gone back to Paris?' Mrs Van Dorman broke into his thoughts.

Monsieur Pamplemousse nodded.

'You're sure?'

'Positive.' Doucette had a horror of unclean sheets. She wouldn't be happy until she was back home again.

'I couldn't help overhearing most of what was going on. I was petrified she might look inside the cupboard. All my clothes are still there. And what was all that about a bed bug?'

'I'm afraid you will have to ask Pommes Frites. He has swallowed it.'

Mrs Van Dorman took the hint.

'So what happens now—aside from wanting me to keep quiet?'

'First I shall get out of these clothes. Then I intend taking a long, leisurely bath. I need time to think. After that I shall get dressed again.'

'The first two shouldn't be a problem, but I can't help much with the third. Unless you fancy using one of my track suits. You're welcome. But without wishing to be rude, it could be a tight fit.'

'There is another way round the problem,' said

147

Monsieur Pamplemousse. 'You could go to my room and get a change of clothing for me.'

Mrs Van Dorman looked dubious. 'I don't see how. If the guard is still in the corridor outside . . .'

Monsieur Pamplemousse picked up his keys. 'There are precedents. What has been done once can be done a second time. Especially if I show you how.'

'If anyone had told me two days ago,' said Mrs Van Dorman, 'that I'd be taking a crash course in lock-picking, I'd have told them where to go.'

'And now?'

'Go ahead. I'm all yours. This whole thing is like a bad dream anyway.'

'Le première leçon,' said Monsieur Pamplemousse. 'Do not be put off by something which looks more complicated than it actually is. The point about locks is that although very often the key may look elaborate, the basic mechanism of the lock itself is really very simple. Much of the design centres on preventing any key other than the correct one from operating it. This is done by building in pieces of protruding metal called "wards" which will stop it turning unless there is a slot cut into the blank in exactly the right place.'

'I think I understand.'

'Here, I will show you.' Taking a sheet of paper and a Biro from the hotel folder on the bedside table he drew out the rough shape of a key. 'The long tubular section fits over the "post" of the lock, that is to say the projection inside the round part of the opening on which the key turns. The flat piece is called the "blank"—until the required cuts are made in it—at which point it is known as the "bit". In essence a skeleton key is an ordinary key with as much cut away from the blank as possible, leaving just enough "bit" to turn the mechanism.'

'Can anybody buy one?'

'If you know where to look. There are books and magazines on the subject. Any crime writer used to doing research would have no problem at all. Failing that, once you know what to do it is easy enough to make up a set yourself. All you need is some blanks, a vice, a hacksaw, some files and a little practice.

'Now, I will show you how to use it.'

Going into the cupboard, Monsieur Pamplemousse slid the dresses to one side and selected a key. He was right first time. A moment later there was a metallic rattle and the lock on the communicating door clicked shut.

'*Voilà!*'

'You've done it before.'

'Now you have a go.' Monsieur Pamplemousse stood back and let Mrs Van Dorman take his place, watching over her as she struggled with the key.

'Take it gently. Not too much force. Try moving it in and out a little and from side to side until you feel something begin to move. Remember . . . I have just locked it. You are trying to unlock it again.'

'Eureka! It works!' Mrs Van Dorman looked as pleased as Punch as the mechanism slid open again. 'How soon before we start lesson two? I see a whole new career ahead of me.'

'Have another go while I run my bath. When you are sure you know how to do it without making too much noise, go downstairs and tell your friend the porter that you want to change rooms. Say you do not like the view from this one.'

Monsieur Pamplemousse crossed to the window and looked out. On the other side of the street immediately opposite him an elderly couple were sitting on a balcony playing cards. They were probably relaxing between treatments.

'It would be a reasonable request. From here you look out on to another hotel. From my side of the hotel there is a view across the whole of Vichy. Ask if room 607 is free. I'm sure they will be understanding. There is almost certain to be a connecting door. It was common practice in the days when this hotel would have been built. There is an identical cupboard in my room.'

'What are you doing?' said Mrs Van Dorman. 'Trying to ruin my reputation? Anyway, supposing 607 isn't free?'

'I didn't hear anyone in there the first night. It is worth a try. The season proper hasn't started, so most of the customers will be passing trade and won't have arrived yet. If it is already occupied we will have to think again. If it is not, see if you can borrow the key to the outside door.'

'If it's that easy, why did someone go to the trouble of breaking into my room through the cupboard?'

'It could simply have been fortuitous. A room-maid may have left the door of the room next to yours open.'

Monsieur Pamplemousse didn't mention the other possibility—that whoever it was hadn't entered via the room next door, but had gone straight to Mrs Van Dorman's. Having discovered the connecting door, he would have opened it to provide an escape route. She could well have disturbed him while he was going through her things. That would explain why the door between the two rooms had been left unlocked. Whoever it was would have wanted to make as quick a getaway as possible. Or even come back in again when the coast was clear.

'Assuming I do manage to get the key to 607, what do you want me to do?'

'Open the connecting door and go into my room. Only make sure whoever is on duty outside doesn't hear anything.

'Apart from a change of clothing, there are things I need. There is a small case belonging to *Le Guide* which may be useful. And on the shelves you will see a set of encyclopaedias. If you can't manage them all, then I would like the one which includes the letter "D".'

'If there is a new guard on duty in the corridor— which is almost certain to be the case—then I suggest that when you leave the room you bring my bags with you. He will assume you are checking out of the hotel.'

Mrs Van Dorman tried the key in the communicating door several times before finally locking it.

She stepped out of the cupboard. 'Here goes. If I'm not back inside half an hour, send out a search party.'

'If you are not back in half an hour,' said Monsieur Pamplemousse, 'I shall come myself.'

Unable to wait for the bath to fill, he added a generous helping of oil, then climbed in and lay wallowing in the running water, adjusting the taps from time to time with his big toe as the bubbles rose higher and higher until they were level with his chin. He hoped the perfume wouldn't linger for days and days. Doucette would have something to say if he arrived back smelling of sandalwood. It must be Mrs Van Dorman's flavour of the day.

As he luxuriated in the water he allowed his mind to wander over the events of the past two days. But for once the warmth, which he had hoped would be conducive to thought, failed to work. He realised all too clearly that apart from Mrs Van Dorman's briefing on the way down and the encounter over dinner, he hardly knew anything about the people involved. Elliott Garner he had spoken to most. Spencer Troon he'd listened to. Harvey Wentworth had struck him as being the most interesting of the five, but that was probably because his leading character was a chef. Sandwiched between two non-speaking actors, Harman Lock and Paul Robard had spent most of the dinner talking to each other.

He tried to remember what Mrs Van Dorman had said about them all on the way down, but he'd been kept so busy the first day—getting dressed for the part of d'Artagnan, trying to picture life in Dumas' time, and if the truth be known suffering 'first night' nerves—and so much had happened since, it was almost impossible.

There was something else hovering tantalisingly in the back of his mind, something he couldn't quite put his finger on. Each time he tried to concentrate his thoughts it disappeared again.

He focused on his watch which he had left lying on its side by the wash-basin. It showed nearly one-thirty. Mrs Van Dorman had been gone nearly twenty minutes. He hoped she was all right. At least he had Pommes Frites to keep guard over him.

Putting thoughts of a leisurely bath to one side, he climbed out, half dried himself, and took one of the hotel dressing-gowns from a rack near the door.

Partly as a means of passing the time, he put through a call to Paris and got the number for the Poison Control Centre. In turn they gave him a contact at the Information Centre in Lyons; a specialist in cyanide.

'You have a pen?'

'*Oui*. Go ahead.'

Once he had established his credentials the information flowed thick and fast.

Most of it only really confirmed what he already knew in a hazy kind of way, and he began to wish he'd waited for Mrs Van Dorman to get back. His Cross pen would have coped better than the hotel Biro, which had seen better days.

Lucrezia Borgia responsible for popular belief that poisoning largely prerogative of women murderers. Medical profession thrown up quite a few in its time . . . on account of easy access, specialised knowledge, etc.

In response to his specific question: cyanide exceptionally quick acting; one of the fastest known poisons. For that reason had been favourite with Nazi criminals and undercover agents . . . cyanide gas used in American gas chambers . . . fatal dose can be as little as 50 milligrams . . . about the same weight as postage stamp . . . that amount gave it ten times more molecules than the total number in human body—whatever that might mean.

He was out of his depth trying to picture it and his wrist was starting to ache. Already he could feel the pain beginning to creep up his right arm.

Paralysis of respiratory centre of the brain causing loss of oxygen. Pulse weakens . . . rapid loss of consciousness. Signs: convulsions . . . coldness of extremities . . . pupils dilated and don't react to light . . . sometimes traces of froth at mouth. Death usually within a few minutes—five at most. When crystals combined with water to produce prussic acid fumes can cause death in as little as ten seconds. Few visible signs . . . skin and body may show irregular pink patches . . . characteristic odour of bitter almonds at

153

mouth. Cyanides quickly altered by metabolic activity once in body, and converted into sulphocyanides which are normally present. Presents problem if no reason to suspect foul play and post mortem not quickly carried out.

Spelling sulphocyanides gave Monsieur Pamplemousse problems of his own and he missed a large chunk to do with ancient Egyptians having distilled cyanide from peach stones, and the fact that Leonardo da Vinci experimented with it until he became an expert poisoner. In his time Leonardo da Vinci had experimented with most things. There were even those who maintained he'd perfected a method of introducing it beneath the bark of trees and then used the fruit to poison one Giangaleazzo Sforza at a banquet in the house of Lodovico il Moro.

Monsieur Pamplemousse gave up writing at that point. He'd had more than enough.

Repeating Ellis's last words produced a loud guffaw at the other end of the line; the first in what had otherwise been a one-sided, not to say sombre conversation. It was quite a plus. The person at the other end didn't sound as though he was normally a bundle of laughs.

Ellis would have done better to have called out for some dicobalt edetate instead of Bâtard Montrachet and fish.

Monsieur Pamplemousse thanked the man for his trouble, then replaced the receiver and sat for a while lost in thought.

At long last he picked up the phone again and made a telephone call to England. He was in the middle of a long conversation when he heard a knock.

'Can you call me back?'

'*Oui*. As soon as possible . . .

'Yesterday would be even better!'

'*Au revoir.*'

Opening the door, he found Mrs Van Dorman standing outside. She was doing a balancing act with his working case and the encylopaedias. Perched precariously on top of it all, looking as though it was about to slide off at any moment, was Norm Ellis's tasting glass. He grabbed it in the nick of time.

'Sorry if I've been a long time.' She sounded out of breath.

'You had a problem?'

'You can say that again. I managed to get the key to the room next to yours, and I didn't have too much trouble with the lock on the connecting door. It was the door itself. It must have been a tight fit to start with, and sometime or other it had gotten itself painted over while it was still shut. It took for ever to get it open.

'Then, when I came out the policeman on duty insisted on carrying everything to the elevator for me. To make matters worse, when it arrived there was someone in there already. I had to go all the way down to the ground floor and bring as much as I could carry in one go up the back stairs. If the desk clerk saw the encyclopaedias he must wonder what's going on. I thought I'd bring the lot just in case.'

While Mrs Van Dorman was talking Monsieur Pamplemousse opened his case and spread the books out across the table.

'Can you manage the rest of the things?'

'I've packed everything in the one bag. One bag! Some people believe in travelling light! How do you manage it?'

'When you spend much of your life on the road,'

said Monsieur Pamplemousse, 'you learn not to waste energy carrying around things you don't need.'

'Touché!'

By the time Mrs Van Dorman returned with his valise Monsieur Pamplemousse was deep into the encyclopaedias. He could have done with Alexandre Dumas' assistant. According to one entry Auguste Macquet had been 'a tireless searcher out of historical documents' on behalf of his master. On the other hand, Auguste Macquet could doubtless have answered the question that was at the back of his mind without resorting to an encyclopaedia.

'I told them I'd decided not to take the other room after all. Who needs a view?'

Mrs Van Dorman laid his clothes out on the bed and then began hanging them up for him alongside her own as though it was the most natural thing in the world.

'Do you really think someone poisoned Norm?' she asked as she draped his jacket over the back of the chair.

'I think there is nothing more certain.'

'Why?'

'If you mean "why do I think it?"—let us just say it is the ex-policeman in me. Instinct tells me I am right. If you mean "why did they do it?" that is something only the person concerned can answer.

'Either way, something must be done. There is always the possibility that a person who kills once will kill again given sufficient reason. I think it nearly happened again last night.'

'You mean the wine?' Mrs Van Dorman gave a shiver. 'If you're right, then it must have been the same person who broke into my room. In which case, he could try again.'

'I think there is nothing more certain.'

'That gives me goose bumps.'

Monsieur Pamplemousse looked up from a list he'd been compiling. 'I don't think you should spend another night on your own anyway.'

If Mrs Van Dorman read anything into the remark she showed no sign.

'But how did he get at Norm?'

Monsieur Pamplemousse handed her his list. 'If you manage to find all these things for me, perhaps I can answer that question too.'

Mrs Van Dorman read the list carefully.

'Are you OK? Do you need a doctor?'

'I am A1, thank you.'

'Then why do you need a thermometer?'

'I have it in mind to test the temperature of the water in the Parc des Sources.'

'If you want a walk—fine. But if you really want to know how warm it is I can save you the trouble.'

Monsieur Pamplemousse looked at her enquiringly.

'It's all in the hand-out.' Mrs Van Dorman crossed to the dressing table and opened a large plastic pack in the shape of a briefcase.

She took out a folder and flipped through the pages. 'Here we are. Célestin comes out at 21 degrees centigrade. In the Source du Parc you have a choice . . . anything from 27 degrees centigrade to 42.5 degrees.' Unfolding the centre pages she spread it out across the table. 'There's a map showing exactly where they are. The Parc de Célestin is down near where we were the other evening . . .'

'May I see that?' Monsieur Pamplemousse took the map from her and studied it intently for a moment or two. The notion that had been nagging at him in the bath had surfaced again.

'Is there something wrong?' Mrs Van Dorman broke into his thoughts.

'You must have a good travel agent,' said Monsieur Pamplemousse vaguely. 'They seem to have thought of everything.'

'Call it American efficiency. It came along with the tickets, an itinerary, and a spare roll of film—compliments of the management.'

'It must have been an expensive operation.'

'More so than average, I guess, but not as bad as it sounds. I gather they've accumulated a lot in the kitty over the past few years. They all chip in with a fixed amount each spring. Besides, they've managed to save quite a lot on the last few trips. When they went to Japan they were guests of some writers' society or other and in return for a mention or two all their expenses were paid for by one of the big electronic companies. Spencer's ill-fated "last breakfast" saved them a bundle; that was eating out on the cheap with a vengeance. This year they were going to the conference at Annecy anyway and I daresay a lot of it goes down on expenses.'

Monsieur Pamplemousse had a sudden thought. 'How about the tasting glasses? Did they come with the other things?'

Mrs Van Dorman hesitated. 'I guess they must have done. They're the kind of firm that thinks of everything.'

She looked at the list again. 'You're sure there's nothing else? I mean, while I'm out you wouldn't like me to get you a kitchen sink? What's a *quincaillerie* when it's at home?'

'A *quincaillerie*,' said Monsieur Pamplemousse, 'is like your travel agent—it is the kind of shop where they have everything. They will help cut the glass for you, and if they can't do it themselves they will know where you should go.'

'I've just learnt something fundamental,' said Mrs Van Dorman. Sarcasm doesn't cross language barriers.'

'*Comment?*'

'Forget it. Seriously—is there anything else you need?'

Monsieur Pamplemousse considered the matter for a moment or two.

'If you come across a good bookshop you might see if you can find any books by our friends down the road.' It was a long shot, but it might tell him something. 'Get as many as possible. And don't forget to ask for *une fiche*.' Madame Grante probably wouldn't wear it, but there was no harm in getting a receipt— just in case.

'You can take Pommes Frites with you, if you like. He could do with the walk. Only make sure you go down the back stairs in case the guard sees you both and puts two and two together.'

'Thanks a heap!' Mrs Van Dorman paused at the door and looked at Pommes Frites. '*Pardonnez-moi.* I didn't mean it. It'll be nice to have someone to talk to. One last question. Why do you need sugar?'

'Let's just say I have a sweet tooth.' Taking the Cross pen from his jacket pocket, Monsieur Pamplemousse twisted the barrel. It was a good 'thinking' pen. He always felt lost without it. 'Talking of which, on the way out could you order me a sandwich and a bottle of wine? I will leave the choice to you.'

'You know something, Aristide,' said Mrs Van Dorman thoughtfully. 'Given time, you could be really infuriating.'

159

As the door closed behind her, Monsieur Pamplemousse picked up the map again and studied it carefully, a slight frown on his face. Turning the pages of the guide until he came to what he wanted, he took a clean sheet of paper from his case and started to write.

The telephone rang once. It was his call from England.

A room-maid arrived with a bottle of Côtes du Rhône and a ham sandwich. While he was eating the sandwich Monsieur Pamplemousse telephoned the Bibliothèque Municipale and had a brief but satisfactory conversation with the head librarian.

He had barely replaced the receiver when Mrs Van Dorman and Pommes Frites arrived back. Pommes Frites looked suitably refreshed and Mrs Van Dorman was obviously feeling very pleased with herself.

'You look as though you have just discovered the wheel.'

She put her shopping down on the bed. 'I feel like I have. Do you want to know something crazy?'

Listening with only half an ear, Monsieur Pamplemousse went through the contents of the bags. He toyed with the idea of telling her his own news, then thought better of it. 'You have done well.'

'Aren't you going to ask me what's happened?'

'*Pardon.*' He gave her his undivided attention. 'Tell me, what has happened?'

'I've solved a mystery. You're not going to believe this.'

'Try me and see.'

'Well, I bumped into Paul Robard while I was out and we got talking. You remember all the hoo-ha over dinner when Spencer Troon pretended he'd been poi-

soned. The cracks he made about having everyone
fooled and how it made him runner-up . . .'

Monsieur Pamplemousse nodded.

'Apparently it all had to do with a wager they'd
made with each other while they were in Annecy. The
first one to come up with a plot for the perfect murder got the jackpot. The catch was that whoever won
it had to convince the rest that his idea would work.
When Norm died everyone assumed at first it was as
a result of a heart attack. Then, as time went on, they
began to wonder if maybe he was trying out an idea
and it had gone horribly wrong. Either way, no one
felt like going into deep mourning and it was tacitly
assumed by all but Spencer that the bet was off.'

'Do you know whose idea it was in the first place?'

'I asked that, but Paul's not sure—he says he thinks
it just kind of happened. Harvey swears it was Norm
himself, which would be rough justice. Harman reckoned he was bugged because they were all getting at
him for pinching their material over the years. Apparently he'd actually had the gall to get up at the conference and deliver a speech on how he thought up
his plots. He even gave a for instance of one he'd
worked out which involved suspending a block of dry
ice above someone while they were asleep. The idea
being that the vapour would flow down and displace
the surrounding air so that the victim would be de-
prived of oxygen and suffocate in his sleep.'

'I'm sure it happens all the time,' said Monsieur
Pamplemousse drily. It sounded like the plot for a
book.

'You can't prove it doesn't,' said Mrs Van Dorman.

He didn't feel inclined to argue. What was the figure for undetected murders? Years ago he'd read a
quote from an American survey. It had been some-

thing like ten to one—and that didn't include deaths classed as accidents or suicides. If you pushed some-one off the edge of a cliff when no one was watching who was to say it was murder?

'Anyway,' continued Mrs Van Dorman, 'it was the start of an argument afterwards because Harvey swore he'd read the same idea in a book and accused Norm of plagiarism. That was more or less how it all began.'

Monsieur Pamplemousse turned the information over in his mind for a moment or two.

'What time are the others leaving?'

'They're booked for New York on the last flight out of Paris. The Air-Inter connecting flight leaves Clerment-Ferrand for Orly at 17.55. I'm catching the same one tomorrow.'

'So they leave here at what time?'

'The car picks them up at a quarter past four.'

Monsieur Pamplemousse looked at his watch again. Fourteen-fifteen. Two hours to go.

'Will you do one more thing for me? I'm afraid it will mean going out again.'

'It beats jogging,' said Mrs Van Dorman. 'I haven't had so much exercise in years.'

'I think the time has come when we should put out some bait,' said Monsieur Pamplemousse. 'I think be-fore the others leave you should go to their hotel and wish them *bon voyage.*'

'I planned to do that anyway. Apart from Paul, I haven't seen them since the dinner.'

'Good. In that case, while you are there perhaps you would be kind enough to give them my felicita-tions and apologise for the fact that I cannot be with them in person. Tell them I am busy; that something has come up over the death of Ellis. Say I have made an important discovery and I am writing out a report in my capacity as an ex-member of the Paris Sûreté. At the same time you can let slip the fact that I am working alone here in your room and do not wish to be disturbed.'

'Putting it out for the cat and seeing who comes to lick it up?'

'Something like that.' He must try and remember the phrase to add to the Director's collection. 'I suggest you take Pommes Frites with you again. He will make sure no harm comes to you.'

'How about you?'

'I shall be all right. It is better that I am seen to be entirely on my own.' It also occurred to him that it was probably better if Mrs Van Dorman wasn't.

As they left the room Monsieur Pamplemousse caught Pommes Frites' eye. Pommes Frites was endowed with extra-sensory perception when it came to summing up situations, and he was wearing his enigmatic expression. It would have been nice at that moment to know what he was really thinking.

The knock on the door came even sooner than he had expected. It was followed by the sound of someone trying the handle. Purposely leaving his papers spread out across the table, Monsieur Pamplemousse crossed to the door and opened it.

'Entrez.' He stood to one side, allowing room for his visitor to squeeze past. *'Comment ça va?'*

'I'm OK. I hope I'm not disturbing you. DiAnn said I might find you here.'

'Please take a seat.' Monsieur Pamplemousse motioned towards a chair.

'I won't stop, thank you. I have a plane to catch. I

163

really only dropped by to say *au revoir* and to ask if you enjoyed the other evening.'

'I could hardly fail to have done. As a meal it was an exercise in sheer gluttony, but there . . .'

'I've heard tell the Romans had a similar dish—the Trojan roast pig. They stuffed it with fig-pickers, thrushes and oysters. In the end their Senate banned it on the grounds that it was too extravagant.'

'In that case, I am even more privileged than I thought.'

'You've read Alexandre Dumas' original recipe for *Rôtie à l'Impératrice*?'

'I am working my way through *Le Grand Dictionnaire de Cuisine*. I dip into it when I go to bed at night, but in a very random fashion.'

'Well, I guess it's a bit like the house that Jack built. The chef starts off with an olive from which he first removes the stone, replacing it with an anchovy. The olive is then placed inside a lark, the lark inside a quail, the quail goes into a partridge and the partridge into a pheasant. The pheasant then goes inside a turkey, which is finally placed inside a suckling pig.'

Monsieur Pamplemousse listened patiently. He could hardly do otherwise. But he was beginning to wonder where the conversation was leading. 'It was a triumph for the *Rôtisseur*. To have cooked such a combination to perfection cannot have been easy.'

'You know what Dumas said about the dish?'

'Tell me.'

'The true gourmet discards the meat. He eats only the olive and the anchovy.'

'It sounds remarkably like yet another of Monsieur Dumas' extravagant statements,' said Monsieur Pamplemousse. 'Sadly, like many of his pronouncements we shall never know the truth.'

'On the contrary. After you and DiAnn left the other night the rest of us paid a visit to the kitchen and managed to rescue the olive from under the very noses of the staff before it disappeared along with the rest of the remains.

'And now, at DiAnn's request, and out of respect for a true gourmet, that is what I have brought you . . .' Monsieur Pamplemousse found himself being handed a small jar '. . . a present from us all before we return home.'

Unscrewing the cap, he put his nose to the opening. Shrivelled though the olive was from the cooking, the smell was redolent with all that had gone into the *Rôti à l'Impératrice*; the rich juices from the pork combined with the ripeness of a pheasant which must have been hung until the feathers practically fell from its breast—it was a wonder the bird had held together when they stuffed it inside the turkey—and that in turn mingled with the smell of partridge, quail and lark. Above it all there was the unmistakable pungent odour of anchovy.

'It is most kind of you. A very great honour. But I cannot be the only one to benefit. I insist that you share it with me.'

'In no way. It's for you. Besides, there's hardly enough to share.'

'In that case, perhaps you will join me in a toast?' Monsieur Pamplemousse went into the bathroom and returned a moment later with a second glass into which he poured the remains of his wine. It was young and crystal clear and he allowed the bottle to drain.

'You know what they call that final drip? The *larme*—the teardrop.'

'You French always have a word for it, right?'

'*Oui, c'est ça.*' He handed over the glass.

'Your good health, Aristide.'

'*A votre santé.*'

Monsieur Pamplemousse sipped a little of the wine, then picked up the jar again. He gazed reflectively at the contents for a moment or two. Then, placing it to his lips, he threw his head back, uttering a sigh of contentment at the thought of the unique pleasure to come.

Conscious that his every movement was being watched, he closed his eyes and allowed the contents of the jar to rest in his mouth for a while, prolonging the experience before slowly beginning to chew, savouring each and every morsel until the very last had disappeared.

'I guess that was something else again, right?'

Monsieur Pamplemousse opened his eyes and was about to reply when a sudden change came over him. The ecstatic expression on his face changed into a look of agony. His breathing became short gasps. The jar slipped unheeded from his hand as he clutched at his throat. Choking, he turned and clutched desperately at the bedclothes, pulling them with him as he fell to the floor. The convulsions lasted at the most a matter of five or six seconds before he gave one final shudder and then lay still, tongue protruding, eyes wide-open and staring.

The long silence which followed was eventually broken by the faint click of the door being closed.

The sound of footsteps disappearing down the corridor had hardly died away when he heard the rattle of a key in the lock and a moment later felt a faint draught of cool air on his face as the door was opened.

Monsieur Pamplemousse waited a moment or two,

then opened one eye tentatively, but he was too late—his second visitor had vanished without uttering a word.

It was several minutes later that the phone rang. He recognised the desk clerk's voice.

'*Monsieur* . . .'

'*Oui?*'

The man sounded taken aback. 'Monsieur is all right?'

'*Oui.*'

'We received a telephone call a moment ago saying that you had been taken ill.'

'As you can hear I am perfectly well.'

'*Monsieur* has no need of an ambulance?'

'No need whatsoever,' said Monsieur Pamplemousse. 'It must have been a hoax. But thank you for calling.'

He replaced the receiver. A hoax? Or someone with a guilty conscience at having left him to his fate. Harvey, or his second visitor?

Mathematically, the permutations were limited, but emotionally . . . emotionally, he needed time to think.

8

THE BALLOON GOES UP

THERE WAS BRIGHT YELLOW GORSE EVERYWHERE and fields carpeted with buttercups, exactly as he had promised there would be when they were driving down from Paris. It was another cloudless day and the sun sparkled from a myriad tiny mountain streams. Every so often they rounded a corner and a totally new landscape came into view. Here and there he spotted the remains of a broken-down shepherd's hut on a distant hillside, but the higher they went the fewer were the signs of civilisation.

After being cooped up in the hotel room for hours on end, the freedom of driving along deserted country roads exceeded all Monsieur Pamplemousse's expectations. He found himself changing gear just for the fun of it.

Slowing down as they reached a piece of straight

road, he opened the car window and took a deep breath.

'You promised to tell me all about perfume one day. Speaking as an expert on the subject, don't you think that is the most satisfactory, the most rewarding scent of all?'

'I wouldn't argue. It's also the most difficult to capture and the most expensive, believe you me. You know what they say—you pay through the nose for perfume. Do you realise it takes a ton of rosebuds to make one kilo of essence? That's a lot of rosebuds.'

'For us at this moment,' said Monsieur Pamplemousse, 'the smell is as free as the air. With all due respect to your last profession, one of the best laws ever passed in France was that which forbade the picking of wild flowers. Left to humanity the countryside would be stripped bare and turned into one enormous car park.'

'I wouldn't argue with that either.'

Anxious not to be left out of things, Pommes Frites stood up on the back seat of the *deux chevaux* and stuck his head out through the opening in the roof, surveying the countryside with a proprietorial air. He, too, gave an appreciative sniff.

'I still can't believe we're here,' said Mrs Van Dorman. 'When I saw you stretched out on my bedroom floor yesterday I'm afraid I panicked. I just ran.'

'You weren't the only one,' said Monsieur Pamplemousse. 'Harvey Wentworth was convinced he'd poisoned me.'

'You're sure you're all right to drive?' Mrs Van Dorman seemed nervous and ill at ease. She glanced down at Monsieur Pamplemousse's wrists. They still showed red marks from the handcuffs.

'The exercise will do them good.'

All the same, a few minutes later he stopped the car and they got out for a moment to stretch their legs. The only sound came from a stream bubbling its way over some nearby rocks. He wished he'd thought to bring a bottle of champagne. They could have sat and talked while it chilled. Even in early June there was still unmelted snow to be seen on the distant peaks. The water flowing down the mountainside would be ice-cold.

'I shall miss all this,' said Mrs Van Dorman. 'Life will seem very quiet on Fifth Avenue.'

'Paris will seem quiet too,' said Monsieur Pamplemousse. 'It always does. Life in the country is really much busier.'

'What things do you miss most?'

'Partly the wildness and the neglect, the crumbling buildings; many of the things which, when I was young, were my reasons for leaving. But France is a big country and each part of it has its own special character and influences. To the south, there is the Italian influence. To the west, that of Spain. To the east, Germany. If I had been brought up in the south I would miss the colour of the roof tiles, or turning a corner and seeing a sun-bleached advertisement for Dubonnet painted on a wall.'

He was glad she had said 'things'. If the question had been more specific, he might have been tempted to give a more direct answer.

'I shall miss the Hôtel Thermale Splendide with its bathtubs,' said Mrs Van Dorman. 'Tomorrow it's back to central heating, air-conditioned apartments, and hotels with sanitised toilet seats.'

'. . . and Monsieur Van Dorman.'

She shook her head, then hesitated for a moment as though weighing up the pros and cons of what to say next. 'There is no Monsieur Van Dorman. There never has been.'

'No Monsieur Van Dorman? Never? How can that be?'

'I guess in the beginning he was a kind of insurance policy; a protection in what was a man's world. I still bring him out from time to time and dust him down. In a funny kind of way he's become part of my life. He's been around so long now I take him for granted. We even have rows sometimes when I want to let off steam. It's like the real thing, but without the hassles.'

And also, thought Monsieur Pamplemousse, without the feeling of having someone else to snuggle up to on a cold winter's night. Perhaps it was part of the price you paid for the benefits of central heating.

'Why did you not tell me before?'

'Would it have made any difference?'

Monsieur Pamplemousse considered the matter for a moment, then side-stepped the question. 'It seems a terrible waste.'

She shrugged. 'It's like we said last night—the night before last—whenever—I've lost track of time; it's a matter of priorities. You can't have everything you want in life. In the beginning my priority had to do with making a career, not finding a husband. First it was perfume, now it's the magazine business. It seemed a good idea to acquire a mythical husband and shelve the problem for the time being. The trouble is, it's the kind of situation that can back-fire. After a certain point if you're not married men wonder what's wrong, and if they think you're married but available, it attracts the wrong sort of person. Anyway, men get frightened by successful women. You can't win.'

171

'I was a little nervous of you at first,' said Monsieur Pamplemousse, 'but for other reasons. At first I thought you were a little *formidable*.'

'More than a little by the look on your face driving down. And now?'

'Now?' Monsieur Pamplemousse went to the car and fetched his camera. 'Now I see you in a different light.'

Crouching down in order to use a low-hanging branch from a tree as foreground interest and to give the picture depth, he framed Mrs Van Dorman sitting on a rock against a background of snow-capped mountains. Hoping she wouldn't notice, he zoomed in for a closer shot and checked the focus. The sun acted as a key-light, picking out the highlights in her eyes. Looking away for a moment under the guise of checking the background, he pressed the shutter release.

'Will you promise to send me a copy?'

'Of course. Although, you may be disappointed. A photograph is the sum of many parts. A split second in time. Often it is the things which are not shown that matter most. The person you are with, where you have just been or where you are about to go.'

'And where are we going?'

'Now? Now I shall take you to a place called Thiers and there, over *déjeuner*, I will tell you everything you want to know. I refuse to talk on an empty stomach. Besides, it is an interesting little town—another side to the Auvergne, and another reason why I left. The people who hanker after the Midi forget the Mistral, just as I often forget that not so long ago, when Thiers supplied France with seventy per cent of its cutlery, the town was full of men who spent their working lives lying flat on their stomachs over the raging

172

streams, their noses literally to the grindstone. They all had a dog lying on top of them. Why? To protect their kidneys from the intense cold. It could have been me; it could have been Pommes Frites.'

'If I say I can't wait', said Mrs Van Dorman, 'it's only because I know I'm going to have to.'

But in Thiers they struck lucky. Feeling saturated from a surfeit of cutlery following a tour of the town, they turned a corner into an alleyway and came across a tiny restaurant. Tucked away behind it they discovered an even smaller courtyard with just three tables set for lunch.

The sun was high overhead and they felt its warmth rising from the paving stones as they took their seats beneath a tree grown tall to escape the surrounding buildings.

Monsieur Pamplemousse ordered a *pichet* of *vin rosé* and while they scanned the brief menu the *patron* brought them a plate of home-cured ham cut into thick slices. He returned a moment later with a basket of freshly baked bread, a bowl of butter and a stone jar filled with gherkins.

Monsieur Pamplemousse chose an *omelette au fromage* and Mrs Van Dorman a *quiche*. While they were waiting they shared a *salade de tomates*.

The omelette, when it came, was exactly as it should have been—*baveuse* in the middle. The *quiche* was filled with egg and ham. There was a plate of *pommes frites*, which they also shared.

For a while they ate in silence. Then Monsieur Pamplemousse, having wiped his plate clean with the remains of the bread, felt inside the secret compartment of his right trouser leg and removed a raisin.

'You're still a believer?'

'Now more than ever, but for a very different rea-

173

son. Yesterday, when I went to your bathroom to fetch another glass, I managed to substitute one for the olive. It got me out of a sticky situation.'

He leaned back in his chair to escape the sun, which had moved round while they had been eating. Recalling the moment, he couldn't help thinking that Glandier would have been proud of him.

'As for their efficacy as a cure for indigestion, I am not sure. Who ever knows if a headache might not have gone away of its own accord without the help of an aspirin? Dumas had a penchant for making statements that were as hard to disprove as they were to prove.'

'Like the storks?'

'Like the storks. He also stated categorically that coffee, far from being the drug we now know it to be, actually served as an antidote to many poisons. I doubt if Monsieur Ellis would have benefited very greatly from the theory—even if he'd had time to test it out.'

'He certainly wasn't calling for coffee when he died,' said Mrs Van Dorman. 'What do you think he did want?'

'I asked myself the same question many times over,' said Monsieur Pamplemousse, 'and on each occasion I gave up because I came to a *route barrée*. In the end I telephoned an old friend of mine, a Monsieur Pickering. He is an Englishman who specialises in crossword puzzles. He has helped me several times in the past. They have very devious minds, the English; they adore riddles. He is also a Francophile and he came up with the answer almost straight away.

'Everyone assumed Ellis had been talking French, whereas Monsieur Pickering's theory is that it was probably a mixture of the two. What those who were present at the time thought he said was "Bâtard Montrachet" followed by *"poisson"*.

'Pickering suggested that Ellis was already fighting for breath through the effect of the poison and that what he might actually have said was: "Bastard!" in English. Then, lapsing into French, he called out *"mon trachée"*—meaning "my windpipe".

'As Pickering rightly pointed out, Ellis unfortunately got his genders wrong. Had he said *"ma trachée"* it wouldn't have mattered. As it was he said *"mon"*, and to any French people around *"mon trachée"*, coupled with the previous word "bastard" sounded like Bâtard Montrachet which, as I'm sure you know, is a white wine from Burgundy.

'Then, when he started calling out "poison", they naturally assumed he was saying *"poisson"* because he wanted some fish to accompany the wine.'

'I don't see what's so natural about it,' said Mrs Van Dorman.

'You are in France,' said Monsieur Pamplemousse mildly. 'Whatever the situation, the thoughts of a Frenchman naturally turn to food. *Par exemple*, do you know the French term for grilling a suspect?'

Mrs Van Dorman shook her head.

'It is called to *cuisinade*. Likewise, the slang for a police van is *panier à salade*. I could give you many more examples. I think Pickering is right. To a Frenchman, Ellis's last words probably seemed a sensible request. One might quibble over his choice— that is a matter of personal taste—but one wouldn't question the sentiment behind it. Besides, until someone has actually died, how is anyone to know they are uttering their last words? To judge from some lines you see quoted, those who speak them must have been polishing and honing them for a long time, and once they have given voice they feel they cannot say another word for fear of spoiling the effect. It is better to be remembered for a stirring phrase like "Not tonight, Josephine" than for something mundane, like "I think I am going to be sick".'

Monsieur Pamplemousse closed his eyes. 'You want to know what I think. The truth is, I don't know, and perhaps no one ever will know the exact truth. Why did someone want to murder Ellis? Who knows? Lots of people probably felt like it. But feeling like it and actually doing it are two very different things.

'My guess, for what it is worth, is that he was the victim of a trick; an elaborate charade which had been carefully planned in advance and which, once the wheels were set in motion, was hard to stop. Perhaps in planning it, the murderer became so involved in the sheer mechanics of the whole thing he lost sight of the moral aspects. One could argue, and if it comes to court, no doubt a good lawyer *will* argue, that in the circumstances "death by misadventure" is the only possible verdict, but my belief is that someone virtually handed Ellis a kit of parts to do the job himself.

'For a while I puzzled over how it could have been done. I pictured a trick glass having being made, one which would have enabled the murderer to conceal cyanide in the bottom, but other than traces of some hard deposit on the inside I could see nothing different about the one you gave me. Besides, having one specially made would have had its dangers, for if whoever did the job got to hear of Ellis's death, as he quite likely would have done, the chances are he would call in the police.

'Thinking about it, I decided it needn't have been as complicated as I first imagined. All the tasting glasses came in the same shape, that is to say they taper towards the bottom. All it needed was a circle of plain glass cut slightly larger than the narrowest point. The poison could be placed in the bottom of the glass—it would require only a minute amount—according to my source less than that needed to cover a postage stamp. The bottom of the tasting glasses is like thick bottle glass, so once the circle was in place any crystals would be scarcely visible to the naked eye. The circular glass could be held in place with something like a sugar solution which, when it set, would be reasonably transparent and yet would dissolve as soon as warm water came into contact with it, thus releasing the glass and the poison.'

'Ingenious.' Mrs Van Dorman looked thoughtful. 'So that's why you wanted to know the temperature in the Parc des Sources?'

'*Exactement*. It also answered another question which had been bothering me. Why a spa? It was the one place where one could guarantee the drinking water would be warm. The deeper the source the warmer it is. I tested my theory while you were out yesterday and it worked.

'As I see it, the argument which took place in Annecy—the wager as to who would be first to plan a perfect murder—were all part of an elaborate and carefully worked out set-up. Once the bait was laid the murderer would have taken Ellis on one side and casually fed him with the bones of the plot, perhaps asking him to treat it as a matter of confidence—which would have been about as much good as asking him to fly. He probably showed him the glass he had already prepared, and then left it lying around anticipating that Ellis wouldn't be able to resist the temptation of swapping it for his own when he thought no one was watching. He judged well. Once they all arrived in Vichy Ellis couldn't wait to unpack before he rushed round to the Parc des Sources in order to try it out.'

'Not dreaming that the crystals in the bottom of the glass were the real thing?' Mrs Van Dorman reached for her sun glasses. 'And you figured that out all by yourself?'

'Not all by myself,' said Monsieur Pamplemousse modestly. 'I could hardly have done it without your help, DiAnn. Besides, for many years I was with the Sûreté. Figuring things out was part of my job.

'As I said earlier, a good lawyer would argue that in stealing the glass Ellis sealed his own fate. In a sense he took his own life. The murderer would plead that he was working on a plot for a book and that in order to make sure it was feasible he had to get all the details exactly right. How was he to know someone would steal the glass? It would also have salved his own conscience to a certain extent. The question then was which of the other five was the culprit?'

'Which is why you got me to put the cream out for the cat so that you could see who came to lick it up.'

'That is so. For a while, given his penchant for writing gastronomic mysteries, I was convinced it would turn out to be Harvey Wentworth. As it happened, one of the books you brought me was by him and it had to do with a man poisoning his wife with cyanide. She took sugar in her coffee and he didn't. He doctored one of the lumps in the sugar bowl with cyanide, so it was only a matter of time before she used it.

'Ellis must have stolen the idea because two years later it surfaced again in a book he'd written under the name of Jed Powers—*Vomit in the Vestry*—a cosy little tale about a homicidal priest who dealt out punishment to his flock by tampering with the communion wafers.

'When Harvey Wentworth appeared clutching the olive and went into his long explanation about why he was giving it to me I was sure I had it right. My guess was that he'd taken fright after hearing that I was actively working on the case and wanted to get rid of me. Then I saw the look on his face as I keeled over and I knew I was wrong.

'What I hadn't bargained for was the cat sending someone else to lick up the cream for him. It was most unfeline behaviour. Perhaps the murderer felt that Wentworth was the only one who might put two and two together and he had in mind killing two birds with one stone. If Harvey Wentworth got himself arrested for my death there's no way he would have got out of it.'

'To think I bumped into Harvey in the corridor as he was leaving,' said Mrs Dorman. 'He must have gone straight back to whoever gave him the olive.'

Monsieur Pamplemousse nodded. *'D'accord.'*

'And Pommes Frites followed him.'

Monsieur Pamplemousse nodded again. 'Other than Harvey Wentworth, Pommes Frites is probably the only one in the world who knows for certain who the murderer is, and there is no way he can tell us.'

He glanced down at Pommes Frites, but Pommes Frites clearly had his mind on other things. He was gazing up at Mrs Van Dorman with a faraway look in his eyes. Perhaps he, too, had fallen under her spell.

'So what's your guess?'

'It isn't so much a guess,' said Monsieur Pamplemousse, 'as an accumulation of arrows, each one pointing in the same direction.

'As I lay on the floor of your room my mind went back to something which had been bothering me ever since I arrived in Vichy. It wasn't until I looked at your map that it began to come clear, and even then it took me a while to grasp the full significance.

'In France, we have a predilection for naming our streets after famous people. In Vichy, for example, your town map lists no less than three hundred and sixty different names. There are four streets called after American Presidents. There is a square Georges Pompidou, a place General de Gaulle, and a rue Napoleon III. There are some streets named after saints, and others after generals, doctors and scientists, from Saint-Barbe to Foch; from Colas to Pasteur. There is even a street named after a seventeenth-century Superintendent of Waters, a certain Docteur Fouet; a worthy man I am sure, and fully deserving of having his name recorded for posterity, but there is no mention whatsoever of a *rue* Alexandre Dumas. I asked myself why? If you have achieved fame as a writer in France and have a connection with a place, however tenuous—you need only have stayed there for a night *en route* to somewhere else—you are assured of a *place* at the very least. Over the years Voltaire has been honoured by the authorities in Vichy, as have Romains and Victor Hugo, but there is no mention whatsoever of Dumas. I cannot think that if he had stayed at the Villa André in order to begin work on a new novel the occasion would have passed unremarked.

'The truth is that the whole episode was a fabrication from start to finish. According to the encyclopaedias Dumas certainly wrote two sequels to *The Three Musketeers*—*Vingt ans après* and *Le Vicomte de Bragelonne*—but I can find no mention of him embarking on a fourth book. I telephoned the library and they had no knowledge of it either, and they should know if anyone does.

'The question I then asked myself was did Elliott dream up the story or was he himself the victim of a hoax? If he concocted the whole thing, then given his pedantic approach and ingrained perfectionism, he must have glossed over the truth for a very good reason.

'Should the matter come to court, and were I appearing for the prosecution, that is an area I would concentrate on. I would put it to him that someone wanted Ellis in Vichy for a very good reason.'

'He certainly did a very good job,' said Mrs Van Dorman. 'He had me fooled.'

'He had everybody fooled. On the other hand, there was no reason why anyone should check up his story. It sounded perfectly authentic, and it would have required a more than averagely erudite Dumas scholar to say otherwise.'

'Where would he have got the cyanide?'

'It is not that difficult. Cyanide turns up in all sorts of different guises. Anyone involved in chemicals can probably get hold of it. As someone once involved in the perfume industry, you should know that. Besides, cyanogenic glucosides are found in lots of natural products—kernels of bitter almonds, apricots, peaches, plums . . . apple seeds. A cupful of apple seeds is known to have been fatal. The leaves from the wild black cherry tree contain amygalin which the stomach converts into hydrogen cyanide. It is used in the manufacture of plastics and as an intensifier in photographic processing. Elliott is a keen photographer.

'If you simply swallow the crystals there is time for

181

treatment. But given the right combination and mixed with water to form prussic acid, a gas is given off and death can take place in a matter of seconds. The one thing which is always present is a smell of almonds, although interestingly a good twenty per cent of people can't detect it.

'By the time we had our dinner Elliott must have had an inkling that I was more than a little interested in Ellis's death. I can only think he must have been trying to throw me off the scent by doctoring the wine with something like almond, suggesting that someone else was trying to poison him. Somehow or other his glass got mixed up with yours.'

'So Pommes Frites' sense of smell wasn't at fault after all?'

'I ought never to have doubted it. As you may remember, he treated the episode of the spilt wine with the contempt it deserved.'

As though to prove his point, Monsieur Pamplemousse picked up the remains of the ham in his fingers and held it under the table. He felt Pommes Frites sniffing it carefully. Then, a moment later, the inspection complete, it disappeared.

'So . . . what are you going to do about it?'

Monsieur Pamplemousse gave a shrug. 'I am a food inspector, not a judge. I comment on the world as I find it—not as I would wish it to be. I shall make out a report and pass it on to the proper authorities—in my position it would be hard to do otherwise, my conscience wouldn't allow it and I have my sleep to think of. After that it will be up to others.'

'What do you think will happen?' persisted Mrs Van Dorman.

Monsieur Pamplemousse repeated his previous 'who knows?' gesture. From the ease with which they

182

had left the hotel that morning he suspected that wheels were already beginning to turn.

'I see endless complications . . . or none at all. The party has already left for America. The authorities will have a field day making up their minds. It will be a matter of looking up the rules . . .'

'Rules?' repeated Mrs Van Dorman. 'Here we are in a country where people happily park on pedestrian crossings or come at you with murder in their eyes if you dare to use one in order to cross the road, and you talk about "rules".'

'That is not the point,' said Monsieur Pamplemousse. 'In truth, France is a country which is steeped in rules. There are rules laid down for everything. Some rules are meant to be obeyed, others are not. The important thing is that when it comes to a disagreement they are there to be referred to. If there is an argument in a taxi about whether or not the window should be open, the passenger has the final say. That is the rule. By the same token, if there is an argument between two passengers on an *autobus* over the same matter, the final arbiter is the driver. That, also, is a rule.

'There is only one area I can think of at this moment which is not governed by rules.'

'And that is?'

Monsieur Pamplemousse picked up the menu. 'Whether to have the *tarte aux fraises* or the *tarte au fromage blanc*. I noticed them both as we came in. The strawberries looked mouth-wateringly fresh— they must be the first of the season. The *tarte au fromage* is a speciality of the region. The Auvergne is known as "the cheese table" of France.'

'Perhaps,' said Mrs Van Dorman, 'we could have one of each and make our own rules as we go along.'

They drank their coffee slowly, savouring each remaining moment.

'All good things come to an end sooner or later,' said Mrs Van Dorman. 'I feel as though I could stay here for ever.'

'I doubt it,' said Monsieur Pamplemousse. 'You would miss New York with its skyscrapers and its way of life, just as I would now miss Paris. Even though there are times when I want to escape, I am always happy to be back there.'

He called for the bill. 'It is my turn this time.'

'If you ever come to New York,' said Mrs Van Dorman, 'I'll take you to the Deli on West 57th. That's something else again. I'll buy you a bagel with cream cheese and lox, or maybe Lukshen Kugel with apple sauce and a potato pancake on the side. Apple strudel and coffee to follow.'

'And when you are next in Paris,' said Monsieur Pamplemousse, 'I will take you to La Coupole for oysters followed by *choucroute*. That, too, is something else again.' He could have listed a hundred other places he would have liked to take her to.

They drove back to Vichy in silence. It was hard to tell what Mrs Van Dorman was thinking behind her sunglasses. Even Pommes Frites was looking unusually thoughtful.

When they reached the hotel a car was waiting to take Mrs Van Dorman on to the airport. Her baggage was already loaded.

She put her hand on his shoulder as they said goodbye. 'I wish you could come as far as Paris—you could wave me goodbye at the airport.'

'I wish I could. But, it is not possible. I have my car.'

'You could leave it. It'll still be here tomorrow.'

'There is also Pommes Frites. He will be lonely without me.'

Mrs Van Dorman gave a mock sigh. 'Excuses.'

'*Raisons,*' said Monsieur Pamplemousse.

'Aristide! *Entrez! Entrez!*' The Director looked to be in an expansive mood as he rose from behind his desk. 'And Pommes Frites. It is good to see you both.

'You have arrived at an opportune moment. The photographs have just come in. A successful operation, by all accounts. It is unfortunate that the pictures taken of you on the *cheval* haven't come out.' He held a strip of negative up to the light. 'It is hard to tell what went wrong. Everything seems blurred. I suspect you must have moved at the crucial moment.'

'I will have a word with Trigaux in the art department, *Monsieur*. He may be able to do something.' Monsieur Pamplemousse didn't add that there was a little private matter he wanted to see Trigaux about too; a matter of some prints of his photographs of Mrs Van Dorman. They should be nearly ready.

The Director crossed to his drinks cabinet. 'I have been going through your report, Aristide. It came through on the fax early this morning. You have done well. A victory over the forces of adversity. It deserves another bottle of Gosset I think.

'I particularly liked the way you ran the flag up the pole, so to speak, and then waited to see who saluted it.'

In acknowledging the compliment Monsieur Pamplemousse also privately had to admit defeat over another matter. When it came to American phraseology, the Director was a clear winner. He also wondered if in watering down his report he'd omitted some essential detail, so that it no longer made sense. In the end he had left out more than he had put in. But the Director was much more interested in peripherals.

'Tell me again about Ellis's last words,' he said. 'I don't want to get the story wrong when I repeat it, and it is too good not to repeat.'

Monsieur Pamplemousse obliged. Doubtless his chief would be dining out on it many times in the months to come.

'I am reminded,' said the Director when Monsieur Pamplemousse had finished, 'of a story my father used to tell me. It is an English joke from the First World War and therefore somewhat convoluted as English jokes often are. It also requires a knowledge of the language and of the somewhat bizarre currency system in use at the time, for it took place long before they had the good sense to become decimalised.

'The message started off as "Send reinforcements, we are going to advance." It was passed down the line by word of mouth and eventually, by the time it reached headquarters, it had become "Send three and fourpence, we are going to a dance." '

Monsieur Pamplemousse laughed dutifully. His old father had told him a similar story, not once but many times.

'Another piece of good news,' continued the Director, as he poured the champagne, 'is that you are no longer on the "wanted" list. My very good friend, the Deputy, has stepped in. Strings have been pulled.'

'I am delighted to hear it,' said Monsieur Pamplemousse. All the way up the *autoroute*, in between listening to a tape of Ben Webster and thinking of Mrs Van Dorman, he'd kept a wary eye on the driving mirror in case he was being followed.

'That is what Deputies are for,' said the Director. 'Without Deputies to oil the machinery from time to time, life would be intolerable. France would grind to a halt.

'Anyway, it wasn't difficult. It seems the man at the farmhouse where you spent the night was running a brothel, catering in the main for the somewhat exotic tastes which are often prevalent in those parts of the world where the winters are long and hard and time hangs heavy. When you arrived dressed as d'Artagnan, brandishing a lady's purse, and wearing *menottes* into the bargain, they not unnaturally assumed you were a new customer anxious to be chastised. It is an establishment popular with the local farming community, some of whom are sufficiently elevated they would rather their proclivities were kept under the bed as it were, instead of on top for all to see. When you failed to give the correct response to a simple code message—something to do with "wanting funny business afterwards"—panic set in. The police were contacted and their first reaction was to throw the book at you. Early reports were somewhat exaggerated. They simply wanted to frighten you enough to make quite sure you never set foot in the area again.'

'I think it will be some while before I do, *Monsieur*.'

'Good, Pamplemousse. I am glad to hear it.' The Director raised his glass. 'I never cease to marvel at the way nature manages to produce a constant stream of bubbles from a point source of such minuscule dimensions.

'Tell me, Aristide, the man's daughters, were they . . . how shall I put it? . . . were they very . . . ?'

Monsieur Pamplemousse sighed inwardly as the Director lapsed into the series of short whistles and

187

other sound effects which he invariably brought into play when he was discussing 'delicate matters'. Clearly, he was not going to accept the plain, unvarnished truth. Embroidery was the order of the day.

'They were not without talent, *Monsieur*. The eldest one sang the Marseillaise while she performed with contra-rotating tassels attached to her *doudons*.'

'*Mon Dieu!*' The Director gave another whistle and then reached for his handkerchief. 'And the others?' he asked, dabbing at his forehead.

'The second one specialised in tricks she had obviously learned in the Casbah.

'The third did amazing things whilst suspended by one leg from a chandelier. They catered for all tastes.'

The Director looked at him suspiciously for a moment, then he rose to his feet and began shuffling the papers around on his desk.

'You look tired, Pamplemousse. I suggest you take the rest of the day off. Put work on the back burner for a while.'

'I was awake for a long time last night, *Monsieur*. I found it hard to sleep after all the excitement.'

'I trust you have no regrets. If you do, I would strongly advise you to go and see Matron.'

'Regrets, *Monsieur*?' Monsieur Pamplemousse raised his eyebrows. 'I think one of my few regrets is that there will be no more Jed Powers books. Or Ed Morgan. I acquired several while I was in Vichy. There are, as they say in the blurbs, quite "unputdownable".'

The Director accompanied him towards the door. 'You will be pleased to know, Aristide, that I, too, have won a minor victory.

'I had an encounter with Madame Grante earlier today. It seems the thespians are causing trouble.

Some of them are claiming extra payment for their performance at the banquet. They claim that when Monsieur Troon pretended he had been poisoned, they were unable to prevent themselves uttering cries of *"Ooooh, la! la!"* and *"Mon Dieu! Mon Dieu!"* Their union says it puts them in another category.

'Madame Grante was in her element. I saw the light of battle in her eyes. All the same, I fear I had to intervene and persuade her to let it go through in return for the exercise of a certain amount of discretion on the other side.'

Monsieur Pamplemousse wondered what life would be like if there were a union of food inspectors. Madame Grante wouldn't know what had hit her if he submitted a claim asking to be recompensed for half the things that happened to him over and above the normal call of duty.

'She is a good sort,' said the Director. 'However, there is one item on your P.39 she is querying. It seems that before you left for Vichy you purchased a large quantity of raisins . . .'

Monsieur Pamplemousse heaved a sigh. Now he knew he was back in earnest.

'If it is of any consolation,' said the Director, 'I have received a very complimentary note from Mrs Van Dorman. I have a feeling she thinks well of you.'

'That is nice to know, *Monsieur.*'

'An attractive lady. I have to admit I fell for her when I was in New York. It is a good thing she is married, otherwise who knows? One evening over a drink she bared her soul to me. Apparently her husband, whom I never met, is of an extremely jealous disposition. He is also an expert in Karate. A Black Belt, I believe.'

Monsieur Pamplemousse had difficulty in keeping a

189

straight face. He was beginning to see the advantages of Mrs Van Dorman's invention.

'Mind you, I would not like to upset her either. She is not a woman to be crossed. There is another side to her character—a hard streak. Not altogether surprising—even in this day and age a woman does not reach the top of her profession without it. I had evidence of it both in New York and again the other evening in Annecy.'

Monsieur Pamplemousse paused for a moment with his hand on the door knob. 'Did you say Annecy, *Monsieur*?'

'I did.'

'You mean Mrs Van Dorman didn't arrive straight from New York?'

The Director looked at him in some surprise. 'Of course not,' he said a trifle impatiently. 'These matters don't just happen, Pamplemousse, as you should know only too well. They require weeks of careful planning. Naturally, as it was her idea rather than Elliott's to hold the event in Vichy, she wished to make absolutely certain everything was going according to plan. She flew into Annecy a couple of days early before coming on to Paris. I joined her there for the first evening to ensure she had all she needed.'

'And did she, *Monsieur*? Have all she needed?' Even as he posed the question, Monsieur Pamplemousse felt his mind racing over the events of the past few days. It felt as though his whole world had suddenly been turned upside down. And yet . . . and yet all kinds of little things began to make sense. It was no wonder Pommes Frites had been giving Mrs Van Dorman some funny looks.

'There was nothing she had not thought of. Everything had been meticulously planned down to the

very last detail—I couldn't have done a better job myself. Brochures, itineraries; she even presented each
member of the party with his own tasting cup in an
initialled carrying case. I need hardly have bothered.
The idea for initiating a competition involving the
plot for a perfect murder was merely icing on top of
the cake . . .'

The Director broke off and looked at Monsieur
Pamplemousse with some concern. 'Is anything the
matter, Aristide? You have gone quite pale.'

'It is nothing, *Monsieur*. A momentary dizziness,
that is all.' Monsieur Pamplemousse pulled himself
together. 'You mentioned another side to Mrs Van
Dorman's character . . . something which happened
in New York.'

The Director glanced uneasily at the door in order
to make sure it was properly shut, then lowered his
voice.

'We were dining *tête-à-tête* at one of those restaurants one normally sees only in Hollywood films. The
sort where they bring a telephone to your table.

'Halfway through the meal Mrs Van Dorman received a call. It gave rise to the most extraordinary
outburst. Not once did she raise her voice, but I tell
you, Pamplemousse, my vocabulary that evening was
considerable enhanced; my grasp of the American
vernacular improved by leaps and bounds. Hell hath
no fury like a woman scorned.

'After she put the receiver down she behaved as
though nothing had happened, but it left me considerably shaken. I honestly believe that for the first time
in my life I was in the presence of a genuine schizo-
phrenic.

'It was only later I discovered the caller was none
other than our friend, the late Monsieur Ellis. He was

191

waiting for her outside the restaurant. She passed it off by saying he had been seeking her advice as an expert on perfume for one of his books—*Charnel No. 5* I think she said it was called. But I was left with the uneasy feeling that there was considerably more involved than that. I beat a hasty retreat.'

'And in Annecy, *Monsieur*? What happened in Annecy?'

'Ah, it was there, Pamplemousse, that I had my original suspicions confirmed in no uncertain manner. Feeling my presence was redundant, I went for a post-prandial stroll round the town. Imagine my surprise, when on the way back to my apartment I saw Mrs Van Dorman entering Ellis's room. I think they planned a "night-cap" together. She was carrying a tasting glass.

'An odd combination, don't you think? One wonders what brought them together in the first place.'

'Perhaps it was loneliness, *Monsieur*.'

'Perhaps.' The Director gave a shrug. 'Now, of course, the question is academic.'

'*Oui, Monsieur*. It is, as you say, *académique*.'

As he let himself in through the entrance door to his apartment block Monsieur Pamplemousse encountered yet another reminder that he was home.

He was about to enter the lift when the *gardien* came out of his office clutching an enormous white cardboard box. He glanced at Monsieur Pamplemousse's luggage.

'It is addressed to you, *Monsieur*, but if you like I will give it to Madame Pamplemousse. She will be back at any moment. She is only out shopping.'

Instinct told Monsieur Pamplemousse to decline the offer. Instinct proved right, as he discovered when he arrived upstairs and opened the box. Anxious to lend a paw, Pommes Frites jumped back in alarm as his master lifted the lid. A large, gas-filled balloon in the shape of a heart floated out and attached itself to the ceiling.

There was card tied to the ribbon. It read 'To my very own Musketeer' and it was signed 'Madame Joyeux'.

Monsieur Pamplemousse read the card a second time, then he detached it and slipped it into his wallet alongside the photograph of Mrs Van Dorman he'd collected from Trigaux. Taking hold of the ribbon, he crossed to the French windows and went out on to the balcony.

He stood for a while lost in thought as the balloon floated across the rue Girardon towards the little park opposite. As it passed over the *boules* area one of the players made a grab for it and missed. He heard the sound of laughter from the man's companions. Further up the hill some children stopped playing for a moment and watched as it drifted higher and higher, gradually losing its heart shape until it was only a speck in the sky.

As it finally disappeared from view Pommes Frites gave vent to a brief but poignant howl and then followed his master back into the room.

With a heavy heart Monsieur Pamplemousse picked up the telephone and dialled a number. He shivered. After the warmth of the balcony the room felt cold and he had little taste for what was to come.

While he waited to be connected he took out his wallet and removed the photograph, laying it out on the table in front of him. It hardly seemed possible that only a few days before he had never set eyes on

193

the face staring back at him. So much had happened since.

'Aristide! You are back!'

Monsieur Pamplemousse jumped. He had been so intent on looking at the photograph he hadn't heard the door open.

'*Couscous!* You startled me.' Rising to his feet he replaced the receiver and held out his arms.

'Who is that?' Doucette glanced at the photograph as she bustled in and set down her shopping.

'She is a colleague of *Monsieur Le Directeur*. I had dealings with her concerning the banquet.' It was no good fabricating a yarn.

'What a strange expression she has.'

'Do you think so?' He took another look. His judgment was clouded by a host of events, but now that Doucette mentioned it there was something odd about the way Mrs Van Dorman was looking. In snatching an unguarded moment he had managed to capture a slightly haunted look; a mixture of triumph and apprehension. And yet, underneath it all there were traces of the warmth he'd grown to know. As a picture it defied analysis.

'If it wasn't for the fact that she isn't your type I would say she is a little in love.'

'Really?' Monsieur Pamplemousse held it up to the light.

'I pity the man whoever he is. She would probably twist him around her little finger, then throw him on the rubbish dump when she'd finished with him.'

Monsieur Pamplemousse eyed his wife curiously. It was the second time in less than an hour that he'd heard the same reservation voiced.

'That is very perspicacious of you.'

As Madame Pamplemousse turned and picked up

her shopping bag she spied the box. 'What on earth do you want that for? We have enough cardboard boxes to last us a life-time.'

Monsieur Pamplemousse slipped the photograph into his pocket. 'One can never have too many, *Couscous,*' he said. 'But if it pleases you I will throw it out when I take Pommes Frites for a walk. He has been cooped up in the car all day and he is a little restive.'

'Don't be too long,' said Doucette. 'I have prepared your favourite stew. It has been simmering all day.'

Monsieur Pamplemousse gave her a quick embrace. It was good to be back.

'You look sad, Aristide. Is anything the matter?'

'Sad?' Monsieur Pamplemousse considered the matter for a moment or two. 'No, just a little disappointed, that is all. Also, I have a report to rewrite.'

'Life is full of disappointments—you are always telling me that.' Madame Pamplemousse pushed him away as she bustled about her work. 'Aren't you going to finish making your telephone call?'

'It can wait,' said Monsieur Pamplemousse. 'I am not sure what I was going to say anyway.' He signalled to Pommes Frites, and Pommes Frites, ever alive to moments when his master was in urgent need of a diversion, obliged with alacrity, making his way towards the outer door.

'And Aristide . . .'

'*Oui?*' He turned in the doorway clutching the box in both arms.

'While you are about it don't you think you should get rid of the rest of your rubbish?'

Outside the apartment block, Monsieur Pamplemousse opened the box under the watchful eye of Pommes Frites and put the label inside. After a moment's hesitation, he added the photograph, stirring

195

the plastic packing with his fingers until both were lost from view. Then he closed the lid, pressing the ends of the sticky tape back into place so that it was safely sealed.

'Allow me, *Monsieur.*' The *gardien* came out of his room and took the carton from him. '*Monsieur* is having *un grand nettoyage*? A spring clean?'

'*Non,*' said Monsieur Pamplemousse firmly. 'It is Madame Pamplemousse who is having *un grand nettoyage*. Pommes Frites and I are going on a balloon hunt.' He gazed up at the sky. '*Entre nous, Monsieur,* sometimes when you throw one up in the air you never know quite where it is going to land.'

These gastronomic mysteries by
MICHAEL BOND
are simply too delectable to be missed!

MONSIEUR PAMPLEMOUSSE

Monsieur Pamplemousse works for *Le Guide*,
France's most prestigious culinary review, and he is
ably assisted by Pommes Frites, a canine with the
tastes of a connoisseur. Pamplemousse is considering giving a restaurant the supreme accolade when
the main course arrives and it is an appallingly
good likeness of a man's head. Suddenly, this food
critic finds his own head on the line when he is
plunged into a case of murder and mayhem and
gastronomic delights.

MONSIEUR PAMPLEMOUSSE ALOFT

An important new dirigible service for Brittany,
France, and Great Britain has been created, and
Pamplemousse must select a menu to reflect the
haute cuisine of Brittany. En route to Brittany, the
intrepid food critic and his dog become entangled
with a travelling circus and a carful of hairy nuns.
A plot is afoot to sabotage the new airship service,
and Pamplemousse must once again save the day.

MONSIEUR PAMPLEMOUSSE INVESTIGATES

Someone is peppering France's most prestigious
restaurant guide with scandal, and it is up to
Monsieur Pamplemousse to find the culprit. *Le
Guide*'s new computer system has been sabotaged,
which might mean delaying publication and endur-
ing much disgrace. Pamplemousse and Pommes
Frites must don some very strange clothes to solve
this puzzle.

MICHAEL BOND

MONSIEUR PAMPLEMOUSSE RESTS HIS CASE
Pamplemousse and his faithful dog, Pommes Frites, are sent to Vichy to attend a banquet for an American mystery writers group. When one of the writers turns up dead, it looks to be the perfect crime. However, the murderer did not reckon on the formidable talents (gastronomic and otherwise) of Pamplemousse and his trusty hound.

MONSIEUR PAMPLEMOUSSE TAKES THE CURE
Monsieur Pamplemousse's doctor has ordered a rest from his calorie-rich diet, so off he goes to a spa with Pommes Frites in tow. However, this spa has a problem. Little old ladies are dying at an alarming rate, and Pamplemousse is determined to get to the bottom of it. And why are there so many sausages at a health spa?

MICHAEL BOND

**MONSIEUR PAMPLEMOUSSE AND
THE SECRET MISSION**
The director of *Le Guide* has a problem. His wife's
aunt runs one of the worst restaurants in France,
and she is demanding to be included in *Le Guide*.
Pamplemousse has a mystery on his hands when he
goes to review this questionable restaurant. Who is
spiking the food with an aphrodisiac of undeniable
potency, and why?

MONSIEUR PAMPLEMOUSSE ON THE SPOT
Monsieur Pamplemousse and his faithful dog,
Pommes Frites, take a much needed vacation in the
French Alps and end up in the midst of an oil crisis.
It seems a visiting oil magnate will give France
none of his precious oil unless he gets a taste of a
special soufflé. However, the dessert chef is missing, and this is a case only Pamplemousse can
solve!